"Snowbird, w...

She whipped back ... arms to keep from bumping into her.

"Keep your voice down!" she scolded in a whisper. "You'll wake the camp with your nonsense!"

She tried to wrench free of his hold, but he held on to her in an amazingly gentle but firm grasp. "Running away isn't going to change how we feel about each other."

Her struggling ceased. "We? I don't recall you asking me how I feel."

He shook his head in denial. "I didn't have to. You tell me with your eyes every time you look at me. A thousand butterflies take flight"—he raised a fisted hand to his chest—"right here."

His closeness challenged her ability to think clearly, so she focused on the fist pressed against his chest and reminded herself a relationship with Marcus would be doomed from the start. He was a soldier, she a Cherokee. Fate had crossed their paths, but it would never lead them in the same direction.

"Say you don't, Snowbird. Look into my eyes and say you don't love me."

I can do that, she thought. If it would put to rest his silly notion that they could have a life together, she could do just that.

Pulling a deep, fortifying breath, she lifted her gaze to his, and the words she intended to say stuck in her throat along with air trying to leave her lungs.

He smiled with satisfaction. "That's what I thought."

Gina Fields is a lifelong native of northeast Georgia. She is married to Terry, a minister, and they have two grown sons who help them in their lawn care and landscape business. Whenever Gina can steal a few minutes out of her busy schedule, she enjoys playing the piano, reading, and gardening. She also enjoys fishing and has even been known to snag the "catch of the day."

Books by Gina Fields

HEARTSONG PRESENTS
HP262—Heaven's Child
HP289—Perfect Wife
HP389—Familiar Strangers
HP411—Spirit of the Eagle
HP432—Tears in a Bottle

Don't miss out on any of our super romances. Write to us at the following address for information on our newest releases and club information.

Heartsong Presents Readers' Service
PO Box 721
Uhrichsville, OH 44683

Or visit www.heartsongpresents.com

Bittersweet Remembrance

Gina Fields

Heartsong Presents

A note from the Author:
I love to hear from my readers! You may correspond with me by writing:

Gina Fields
Author Relations
PO Box 721
Uhrichsville, OH 44683

ISBN 1-59789-036-7

BITTERSWEET REMEMBRANCE

All scripture quotations are taken from the King James Version of the Bible.

All of the characters and events in this book are fictitious. Any resemblance to actual persons, living or dead, or to actual events is purely coincidental.

Our mission is to publish and distribute inspirational products offering exceptional value and biblical encouragement to the masses.

PRINTED IN THE U.S.A.

Dear Reader,

Bittersweet Remembrance *is the follow-up to two other Heartsong titles:* Spirit of the Eagle, *HP411, which was published in the year 2000, and* Tears in a Bottle, *HP432, which was published in 2001. As this third book has been five years in the making, I thought you might benefit from a brief summary of the first two books and how they lead up to this one. I also thought a little bit of history regarding the Cherokee Removal that took place in 1838 and the related actions prior to this agonizing event would be helpful in order for you to understand the characters in this story, particularly the Cherokee and the roles they played in society at this pivotal point in their history.*

In 1828, gold was discovered in northeast Georgia, a region of the state primarily controlled by the Cherokee people. The promise of easy money brought an onslaught of white settlers to the area. These newcomers soon set their sights on not only the gold in this region but also on the land. The Georgia legislature began to petition the United States government for removal of the Cherokee.

In 1830, Congress passed the Indian Removal Act, which would require all Indians living east of the Mississippi to be relocated to land west of the Mississippi. At first the Indians tried to fight the removal legally by challenging the law in the Supreme Court and establishing the independent Cherokee Nation. In 1832, the Supreme Court ruled in favor of the Cherokee, declaring the Cherokee would have to agree to removal *in a treaty, which would then have to be ratified by the U.S. Senate. By 1835, the Cherokee were divided on the issue. Most supported Principal Chief John Ross, who was against the removal. However, on December 29, 1835, twenty Cherokee men met in secret, without the consent of the principal chief or the majority of the Cherokee people, and signed the illegal Treaty of New Echota, which gave the United States government the legal document needed to remove the first Americans from lands they had occupied since before history has record.*

But not all Cherokee left their beloved homeland east of the Mississippi. A scant few rebelled and fled to the Appalachian Mountains. It is those I write about in Bittersweet Remembrance. *In no way do I claim to be able to capture the true picture of heartbreak and loss suffered by the Cherokee people; I only try to tell the fictional story of one family.*

As you read Bittersweet Remembrance, *you will notice the Cherokee characters are a very cultured, well-educated, and peace-loving people. At a time when much of the West was still unsettled, many of the eastern Cherokee had adopted the European-style customs and obtained the knowledge possessed by the white settlers. The Cherokee's willingness to learn the English language and system of education not only allowed them to coexist peacefully with the growing number of settlers in their nation but also to conduct intelligent and profitable business dealings with their white counterparts. At the dawning of the nineteenth century, one of the wealthi-est men in the Western Hemisphere was Cherokee Chief James Vann. His eight-hundred-acre plantation boasted several hundred slaves, forty-two slave cabins, six barns, five smokehouses, a trading post, more than one thousand peach trees, one hundred and forty-seven apple trees, and a still.*

In 1801, at the invitation of Chief Vann, Moravian mission-aries established a missionary school near his home in Spring Place, Georgia. The mission was located on land south of Chief Vann's massive plantation home. The school was built on property and with materials provided by Chief Vann. Chief Vann also offered the help of some two hundred slaves in constructing the school. His home still stands in northwest Georgia today as a historical site and is one of the oldest remaining structures in the northern third of the state.

Bittersweet Remembrance *begins in 1811 at the missionary school located in Spring Place. Snowbird Walker, the daughter of an Irish fur trader and a Cherokee maiden, was sent to Spring Place two years earlier to learn the ways of her white father. There she met Marcus, the son of a Moravian missionary. The two young people fell in love but were separated when Marcus joined the military. Before they could reunite, they were both led to believe the other was dead. However, out of this relationship a set of twins were born to Snowbird—a boy named Ethan and a girl named Emily. Snowbird raised the children alone, never revealing to them the true identity of their father.*

The first book of this series, Spirit of the Eagle, *is Ethan Walker's story and begins at the onset of the Cherokee Removal in 1838. During the days leading up to his flight to the mountains, Ethan meets and falls in love with Lillian Gunter, the young white schoolteacher who teaches the white children who live across the river from Ethan's Cherokee settlement. As the Walker family is about to depart, Ethan learns Lillian's life is in danger and he must rescue her from an evil relative who intends to kill her and frame Ethan for the crime. As a result of the rescue, Lillian must make the journey with Ethan to the Appalachian Mountain wilderness.*

Tears in a Bottle, *book two of the series, is the story of Ethan's twin sister, Emily, a young widow and mother of two. When she ventures outside the mountain valley refuge in search of herbs for her sick child, she is captured by soldiers who are rounding up the Cherokee for the removal and is forced to travel west. This is the journey that would come to be known as the "Trail of Tears" because so many of the Indians suffered and died along the way. During the weeks and months that follow, she falls in love with the kind soldier in charge of the depot she is traveling with. The couple marries and feels led to establish a church in the new western Cherokee territory.*

Now it is time to finish the love story between Ethan and Emily's parents, Snowbird and Marcus, which started twenty-seven years earlier at a mission school in northwest Georgia. I hope you enjoy Snowbird and Marcus's story. But most of all, I hope you see that God's love can cover the greatest of sins and warm the coldest of hearts.

Love and blessings,
Gina

prologue

Snowbird tiptoed into the herb garden of the missionary school at Spring Place, Georgia. She padded along the outer row where fruit trees shadowed her, protecting her from being seen in the light of a high half-moon and of the countless pinpoints of starlight sprinkled across the deep blue velvet sky.

The scent of blossoming fruit trees flavored the air with mouthwatering sweetness. Only the whistle of a distant whippoorwill and the hoot of a lone owl broke the quiet of the balmy May night. The grass was soft and silent beneath the binding slippers she wore. She much preferred the single-seam ankle moccasins her Cherokee mother had taught her to make. But here at Spring Place—a world ruled by the white man—anything that symbolized her Indian heritage was forbidden.

As was her love for a white man.

She ducked beneath a tree limb. Three years ago, her white father had brought her to the school. He had wanted her to acquire the education of his people, but she had wanted nothing to do with the staunch academy or the prudish missionaries who looked at her in her buckskin dress like she were a wild animal in need of skinning.

And skin her they did. At least, that's what it felt like to Snowbird.

The missionaries' wives had replaced her beloved buckskin with pantaloons, corsets, dresses of spun cotton, and shoes that pinched her toes. The long black hair she'd worn loose or in a single braid down her back, they'd pinned up into a tight bun she detested.

For two years, she'd rebelled. She would intentionally tear her skirts on thorns, step into mud puddles after each rain, and snag her hair on low-hanging tree branches until the pins fell out. She was tenacious—and successful—in her determination to cause the missionaries grief.

Then Marcus came, and everything changed.

She never would forget the day he came riding up to the mission, seated beside his father on the bench of a supply wagon. Marcus was a lanky boy of sixteen then—two years her senior—with startling blue eyes and hair that shone like dark gold in the sun.

He couldn't seem to take his eyes off of her.

A warm smile touched Snowbird's lips. A tiny seed had been planted that day, a young and tender kernel that had grown into something wild and beautiful.

Her thoughts caused her breath to catch in her throat. Just last month, Marcus had asked her to marry him. He'd soon finish school, step onto the missionary field and out from under the control of his father, who thought his son above marrying a half-breed. She and Marcus would finally be free to wed.

Sometimes it amazed her that Marcus would actually defy his narrow-minded father and marry her. Reverend Nathaniel Gunter was a very dominating man.

But Marcus was much stronger than his father, in a quiet, steady way. Like the solid, silent Appalachian Mountains that had always been her home. And that was only one of the reasons she loved him with every breath she breathed.

She swept aside the stringy branches of an aged weeping willow and ducked inside the tree's protective dome. The moonlight sliding through the spindly branches threw a mottled patchwork of light across the ground. As the limp branches swayed back into place, moon fairies danced around her feet like delicate bridal lace swaying in the wind.

She did not see him at first, but she felt him. The power of his presence raced across her skin. Her breathing heightened, then ceased. Her palms itched with anticipation.

Then a shadow slid from behind the tree's trunk. With lungs full of trapped air, she watched his silhouetted frame glide through the crystalline prisms of the night's light.

As he stepped up to her, the burning in her ribs forced her to breath. Alluring scents—the crispness of his recently laundered shirt; the herbs he'd used to wash his thick, wavy hair; the soap clinging to his skin—filled her senses with a need to be closer to him, to feel his arms around her.

Reaching up, he brushed the backs of his fingers across her cheek. "Mary," he said, just above a whisper.

She had always preferred "Snowbird," her Cherokee name. But the way Marcus said the name the missionaries had given her, in a voice that had recently taken on the velvet edge of maturity, quelled the sharp arrow of resentment she once felt whenever another spoke her white name. She closed her eyes, and like a strong wind at her back, the forces of nature urged her forward.

He slipped his arms around her waist. She lifted hers to

circle his broadening shoulders. Resting her head against his chest, she listened to his strong, steady heartbeat.

"Oh, Marcus, I have missed you so." Even though they saw each other every day on the school grounds, it wasn't the same as being alone with him, having him hold her this way. "I don't know what I'd do if we didn't have these rare moments."

In a quick, jerky motion, his arms tightened around her. With one hand, he smoothed her hair. Then he went deadly still, igniting an unsettling spark of foreboding deep inside her. Something was wrong; she sensed it in the way he held her. For a long time, neither of them spoke.

"I love you, Mary," he finally said. "You know that, don't you?" His words and tone, both filled with dread, sounded like the prelude to good-bye.

A wave of panic rolled through her, but somehow she managed a nervous-sounding laugh. "Of course I do."

Another strained and heavy silence followed.

She slid her hands to the front of his shoulders and leaned back, looking up at him, wishing she could see his eyes, read the silent message there. But shadows cloaked his face. "What is it, Marcus?"

He ducked his head. "I–I've joined the army."

His words circled her mind several times before settling; then a soft, incredulous, "The army?" slipped past her lips.

Another pause then, "Yes."

Frowning, she blinked. This couldn't be right. She and Marcus had never discussed him joining the army. Never. She stepped back, breaking contact. Confusion marred her mind. A razor-sharp pain pierced her. Crossing her arms, she turned away. "That's a rather critical decision for a man to make without informing his future wife, isn't it?"

"There was no time. We haven't been able to meet for over two weeks, and I wanted to be alone with you when I told you."

Why? she wondered. So she wouldn't cry like a spineless weakling in front of the others like she was about to do now? She clenched her teeth, swallowing the tears burning her throat. The army meant he would be leaving, that they would be separated for months at a time.

Another thought slipped unbidden into her mind. Had his feelings for her changed? Was that why he hadn't told her before now?

"What about us?" Her voice trembled.

Hands settling on her shoulders, he urged her to face him. "I did this for us, Mary. I'll finally be out from under my father's control—not have to depend on him to feed me and put a roof over my head." His voice rang with both pride and anticipation. Gently, he squeezed her shoulders. "He can never come between us again. We can finally be married and start our life together."

She laid a hand against his chest. A rapid pulse of excitement tapped her palm. But her emotions were mixed. His announcement had taken her by surprise. Struggling to quell her shock, she asked, "What about school? What about your plans to become a missionary?"

"Those were my father's plans," he replied, the sharp edge of bitterness flattening his tone. "But I've finally convinced him I could never be an effective missionary because my heart's not in it, and God has never really impressed me that the missionary field is where I should be. For some time now, I've felt I could better serve Him on the battlefield."

Battlefield!

The reality of his words crystallized in her mind. He would

be risking his life frequently for the United States, a country with many more battles to fight in its effort to lay claim on land now occupied by others, including her own people.

Before she could further protest his decision, he laid a hand on the side of her face. "Mary, the only thing I want more than to be a soldier is a life with you." His thumb caressed her cheek. "If you ask me not to go, I won't."

All the feelings of hurt, anger, and betrayal his announcement had spawned dwindled down to one single emotion—guilt. How could she deprive him of something he wanted so much?

Besides, if he backed out now, he'd feel like a deserter, someone who had abandoned his duties to his country. And he could never live with that. He was too honorable.

"When do you leave?" she forced herself to ask.

At least five agonizing seconds passed. "Tomorrow."

"Tomorrow!"

"I'm afraid so. I'm going back with Captain Davis, the gentleman who's been visiting with us this past week, and he must leave in the morning. But I'll come back for you when I have my first leave, which should be before Christmas. I'll have a little money saved by then and can put a roof over our heads."

Conflicting emotions clashed inside her: sadness that they would be apart for a time and joy that they could finally plan their future.

Grasping his shirt as if she feared he would vanish, she leaned into him. "Hold me, Marcus. Hold me until you must let me go."

"Of course, my Mary," he whispered. Then, slipping his arms around her, he kissed her like he never had before.

one

June 1838
North Carolina Mountains

Dear Marcus,
  I know this letter will come as a surprise to you after all these years. But a cruel twist of fate has fallen upon our children, and for their sakes, I felt it necessary to contact you.
  First of all, let me assure you that your daughter is safe. She is among friends who care deeply for her.
  Now having said that, I will explain my reason for writing this letter. However, to do so while avoiding confusion, I must go back in time—to Spring Place.

Snowbird Walker paused in writing and gazed through the opening of her buckskin shelter. Although the sky was cloudless and the moon full, she saw nothing of her primitive Cherokee village beyond the yellow light of the tallow candle sitting in a clay saucer beside the worn blanket she sat on. But her mind's eye painted the obsidian curtain of night with images of another place, another time, and bittersweet memories of the past.

Spring Place had been where she had met and fallen in love with Marcus Gunter. It was there he had vowed to love her forever. It was there he'd asked her to marry him. And it was there he'd left her.

Her throat tightened. She had been so naive then, so blinded by their forbidden love.

She raised her empty hand to her aching chest and grasped the front of her homespun blouse. An idle tear trickled silently down her cheek. If only she had known what tragedy her secret would one day bring, she would not have harbored it for so long—and her son would not be suffering such loss.

Her thoughts led her back to the task at hand. Wiping her face with the back of her hand, she drew in a deep, steadying breath. Then, with the heavy heart of a mother who had caused her child great pain, she dipped her feather pen in the inkwell and continued to write.

> *Shortly after you left Spring Place to join the army, I learned I was with child. Two days later, your father told me you had been killed during a training exercise. Of course, I believed him. I had no reason not to.*

Her hand continued to glide across the parchment. She wouldn't allow herself to stop and dwell on the lie that had driven them apart or to feel the sting of rejection that sometimes still plagued her.

> *I did not tell your parents of my condition for fear they would shun me, deny the child was yours, or take the baby from me after I gave birth. So I returned home to my family. Seven months later, I gave birth to twins.*
>
> *That's right, Marcus. We have two children together: a boy, Ethan, and a girl, Emily. Both are strong and healthy adults now. Ethan has your eyes.*

A faint smile touched Snowbird's lips. Quickly, she banished it and drew her mouth into a thin, determined line. She could not allow her affection for her children to weaken her composure. Oftentimes, unrepressed emotions uncovered things better left buried. And she never wanted Marcus to know how much his leaving her had hurt her—or how long it had taken her to get over him.

She wanted the letter to sound cordial but detached. Exactly how she intended to react when she saw him again.

We also have two grandchildren. A boy and girl—six-year-old twins belonging to Emily.

Ten years ago, when your sister and brother-in-law moved to Adela, Georgia, the town that was once part of my people's village, I learned you were alive. As you know, I never had opportunity to meet your older sister when I lived at Spring Place as she was already married then and living away with her husband. So she never knew of the relationship you and I had had, and of course, I never told her. The twins were sixteen then, and you were happily married with a young daughter. I figured to tell you about our children then would only disrupt our lives and cause uncomfortable, possibly resentful feelings between our families. So I have remained quiet about the children's paternal parentage until now.

As you are well aware, the enforcement of the Treaty of New Echota is forcing my people west. However, certain members of my clan chose to remain in the East. To do so, we have had to find a safe place to hide until the antagonism over the forced removal settles and we can once again pursue our freedom. We have found that place in a valley high in the Appalachian Mountains of North

Carolina. We call our new home the Blue Haven.

Three months ago, several of us came to the Blue Haven to begin preparing the land for those of us who would need a place of refuge during the removal. Ethan was to stay at our home in Georgia with the rest of the family, gather supplies, and come later. Only, when he did, it was with a new bride. . .your daughter.

Oh, Marcus, our son has married your daughter, his half sister.

Snowbird paused, blinking past a stinging blur. Of all the tragedies her sin had brought upon her, this one was the worst, for it had caused unbearable pain to one of her children.

Drawing in a shaky breath, she steadied her determination. Her eyes burned, her throat ached, her heart hurt. But she must finish the letter. The sooner Marcus learned what had happened to his daughter, the sooner he could come and get her, and everyone could move on.

And while the once-close relationship between Snowbird and her son would be forever tarnished, he would one day realize, as she had, that in spite of pain, tragedy, and sorrow, life did continue on.

They were so happy when they arrived in the valley, one would have thought they were made for each other. But when I learned Lillian's parentage, I had no choice but to tell them the awful truth.

Both Ethan and Lillian were devastated to learn they are so closely related. And I fear Lillian, being a newcomer to our village and surrounded by people she knows little of, will fall into an irreparable depression.

*She needs you, Marcus. If there's any way possible, please
come. I cannot tell you how to get here, but your brother-in-
law, Frederick, can show you. He knows the way. He knows
everything about my family except that you are the father of
our children.*

*I trust you will make haste, Marcus. I will anxiously await
your arrival.*

Snowbird Walker

Snowbird folded the letter, slipped it into a parchment
envelope, and laid it aside. She'd give it to a messenger tomorrow morning to take to a friendly, trusted white man who
would deliver it to Marcus.

She was taking a great risk by sending him this letter, but
her instincts told her Marcus would not reveal her people's
whereabouts to his government. At least not until he found
his daughter and safely removed her from the Blue Haven.
And if Frederick suspected Marcus would lead troops to the
valley, the minister would never show the colonel the way.
So once Marcus left, if Snowbird suspected he was going to
return for her clan, at least they'd have time to relocate.

Knowing sleep would be long in coming this night, she
ducked out of her shelter into the dim stillness of the warm
June evening. The beauty of the star-sprinkled sky, the
peaceful cadence of the night creatures, and the distant gurgle
of a mountain stream seemed to mock her. For inside her
soul, a tumultuous battle raged.

Across the village, silhouetted shelters similar to her own
stood dark and silent except for one: her son and daughter-
in-law's. Tonight they grieved over what they'd lost. Their
hearts lay open, wounded, and bleeding. And the secret she

had kept hidden, the lie she had chosen to live for the past twenty-seven years, had been the weapon that had inflicted their wounds.

If she lived to be a hundred, she'd never forget the pain or the reproach in her son's eyes when she'd told him he'd married his half sister.

A chill raced up her spine, sending a shudder through her. She crossed her arms and rubbed her palms over her upper arms. She'd once thought she'd paid for the sin she'd committed twenty-seven years ago. But it appeared the debt had not yet been satisfied and never would be. For now, she had to live with her son's unforgiveness. . .and with facing Marcus Gunter again.

two

Colonel Marcus Gunter's hand trembled, as did the parchment clasped between his thumb and forefinger. Shock—the kind that came from a crippling blow to one's blind side—paralyzed him. The four walls of his brother-in-law's modest sitting room seemed to close in on him until they were suffocating him.

For two weeks he'd been frantic, worried out of his mind, thinking his daughter had been kidnapped by two Cherokee men rebelling against the forced removal.

For twenty-seven years, he'd thought Mary Snowbird Walker, the woman he'd once planned to marry, was dead.

Relief over learning his daughter was alive and safe tangled with the staggering surprise that Snowbird was alive. And trapped inside that knotted web was the mind-numbing fact he had two twenty-six-year-old children.

In forty-four years, he'd faced his share of unanticipated moments, but none had come close to astounding him like this one. His world tilted, and someone captured his upper arm.

"Maybe you should sit down."

Marcus angled his head and stared through a haze of confusion at his brother-in-law. As Marcus focused on the older man's concerned face, a few of the last words he'd read filtered into his stunned consciousness.

"Frederick. . .knows everything. . . ."

The sharp edge of anger sliced through the fog in his brain.

A spasm locked his jaw. His nostrils flared. The parchment crumpled in his fingers, then fell to the floor.

He grabbed the front of Frederick's white shirt and backed the minister to the wall. "You knew? For more than two weeks, you've let me believe my daughter had been kidnapped, let me search for her—and all this time, you knew where she was?"

Like the window of calm in the midst of a storm, Frederick steadily held Marcus's gaze. "The Walkers are my friends. I did what I had to do to protect them."

Marcus's grip tightened until the taller man's feet almost left the floor. "And Lillian is my daughter," he ground out. "Did you not stop to consider her welfare?"

"I'm sorry, Marcus. Truly I am. Perhaps when you know the whole story, you'll better understand."

Marcus doubted it, especially in his present state of mind.

He forced himself to relax his hold on Frederick, just a little bit. "Did you know Lillian was married?"

Frederick swallowed. "Yes. I performed the ceremony two weeks ago."

Another surge of anger jolted Marcus, and sheer willpower kept him from shoving his brother-in-law through the wall.

"Frederick. . .knows everything. . .except that you are the father of our children."

The words rolled around his mind like boulders tumbling downhill. So Frederick didn't known the secret Snowbird had lived with for so many years. Nor did he know the secret Marcus had carried for two decades—a deception he'd lived in order to protect his daughter.

And now the charade he'd played had come back to haunt him. What would Lillian do, how would she feel about him when she found out the truth?

Concern over her well-being took precedence over everything else. Frederick had plenty of explaining to do, as did Marcus, but it would have to wait until they were on the trail. Right now, his priority was getting to his daughter—and the man she'd married, his son—as quickly as possible.

Releasing his brother-in-law, Marcus stepped back. "Ask Emma to pack us some food for our journey," he said, referring to his sister. "We leave within the hour."

✥

That night, Marcus sat, elbows on knees, hands wrapped around a cooling tin coffee cup, staring at the small fire he and Frederick had built more for light than for heat. Even though the dew had long fallen, the night air in the Appalachian foothills was still warm and sticky. The Southeast had been gripped this year by a ruthless drought unwilling to let go of the land.

The two men had ridden fast and hard that day, stopping only when Frederick insisted the darkness posed a serious risk to the horses. Marcus hadn't wanted to stop, even though he knew what Frederick said was true. The deeper into the Appalachian Mountains they traveled, the thicker the foliage that hid the deep crevices, small animal dens, and sharp rocks that threatened both man and animal even in daylight. So Marcus had agreed to stop until first light of dawn.

The fire crackled softly. Dancing flames spat an occasional spark into the darkness. The rhythmic trill of night creatures filled the air with a monotonous, high-pitched song that echoed inside Marcus like the thunder of an approaching storm. How was he going to make it through the four- to five-day journey to the Blue Haven, knowing his daughter and the son he'd never met were suffering because of a choice he'd made years ago?

"I know you don't understand why I did what I did, Marcus."

Marcus didn't immediately respond to Frederick's statement. The colonel did feel betrayed by his brother-in-law, but at the same time, he understood why the minister, knowing Lillian was safe, would hesitate to reveal her whereabouts in order to protect his Cherokee friends.

In December of 1835, several prominent Cherokee men had taken it upon themselves to sign a bogus treaty exchanging the eastern Cherokee lands for lands west of the Mississippi. The deal was sealed without the knowledge of their Principal Chief John Ross or the majority of the Cherokee nation. In turn, the U.S. government had upheld that illegal treaty and was now enforcing it. Federal troops, under order of the president of the United States, had been moved into the Cherokee nation to remove the Indians who refused to leave their homeland willingly.

When Marcus had received his orders to assist in the removal, he'd requested he be allowed to set up the fort under his command near Adela so he could be near his daughter. She had moved from their home in Virginia to Georgia three months earlier to live with his sister and brother-in-law and teach school in the small gold-mining town in northeast Georgia.

Before Marcus had been forced to leave his post under charge of his second-in-command in order to search for his daughter, he'd witnessed the heartbreak and devastation of the Indians being taken from their homes, marched to the holding forts, and forced to live in the crowded, filthy stockades. Disease rampaged through the camps. Numerous graves began to the spot the hillsides.

What man wouldn't help his friends escape such abominable conditions and treachery if he had the chance?

Marcus heaved a relenting sigh. Only one without honor, he had to acknowledge.

"If it's any consolation at all, Marcus, Lillian is very happy with Ethan," Frederick added. "She made the choice to go with him even when he tried to get her to return home with me." He paused as though to let the words take root, then added, "They love each other very much."

Frederick had not read Snowbird's letter and was puzzled, Marcus was sure, over why she'd written it, thus revealing the whereabouts of her people to an army officer who was duty-bound to enforce the removal treaty. Since Marcus had been more focused on riding today than on talking, the minister still didn't know Ethan was Marcus's son.

And while Marcus wasn't inclined to talk about it at the moment, he couldn't find a reasonable excuse to put off telling his brother-in-law why Snowbird had taken such a risk in contacting him.

He glanced over to where Frederick sat a few feet away, his position matching that of Marcus. "There's something I need to tell you, Frederick. Something I learned just this morning, when I received Ma—" He bit back the last syllable. He'd always called Mary by her white name. But she now referred to herself as "Snowbird," the name given to her by her Cherokee mother. And Marcus wasn't sure Frederick knew her by her white name. "When I received Snowbird's letter," Marcus corrected.

A suspenseful silence hung between them, lasting only a few seconds, but it felt like long, anxious minutes.

"Ethan Walker. . .is my son."

Frederick's expression remained unchanged for a moment, as if the words Marcus had just spoken hadn't reached the older man's hearing. Then the minister blinked. "What did you just say?"

"I said, 'Ethan Walker is my son.' His twin sister, Emily, is my daughter."

Frederick gave his head a slow, incredulous shake. "I don't understand."

Staring down at the tin cup trapped between his hands, Marcus sighed. Suddenly he felt tired. The muscles in the back of his neck and shoulders ached with worry. "Snowbird and I attended school together at Spring Place," he explained. "We were friends at first; then we fell in love. I asked her to marry me when she was fifteen and I was seventeen, but my father was strongly opposed to the match. He said we were too young and that marriage to a woman of mixed race would make us and our children a target of prejudice. He went as far as to say that he would disown me if I went through with the marriage." But Marcus had never told Snowbird that. He'd hoped that his father would eventually come to love her as much as he.

A sour feeling stirred in the pit of his stomach. He had given his father far too much credit.

"I joined the army so I could make a life for us," he continued. "I planned to return home on my first leave, marry her, and find us a home close to where I was first stationed."

A hot flood of a memory slammed into Marcus's chest, a fierce pain he hadn't felt in years—not even in the wake of his wife's recent death. "When I returned home, my father told me Snowbird had died of the fever. He even took me to what was supposed to be her grave." The heat rose to his throat, threatening to choke him. "Apparently, he lied."

So there it was, the cruel truth—at least part of it. "We were together. . .intimately. . .once, the night before I left to join the army." Closing his eyes, he thought of all the memories he'd missed, the years he'd lost. "For twenty-seven years, I thought she was dead. Never once did I suspect she might be alive. . .or that we had children."

"Marcus. . ." Frederick's voice was raspy with emotion. "I didn't know."

Marcus heard the self-recrimination in his brother-in-law's voice, sensed the minister thought himself to blame.

Opening his eyes, he met Frederick's confused and bewildered gaze. "You wouldn't know. You and Emma had already married and had moved away when we moved to Spring Place where Snowbird attended school. You never met her. . .until you moved to Adela." A laugh laced with cynicism left Marcus's chest. "What a strange twist in fate, that you and my sister would move next door to the woman I once loved and planned to marry. . .and the children I didn't even know existed."

Marcus turned his gaze back to the dying fire. Words ceased for a small space in time, but the night creatures continued to sing, each swell of their cadence throbbing inside Marcus's head.

"This means. . .Lillian has married her half brother," Frederick said, as though he'd just been handed down a death sentence. His eyes slid shut as he whispered a desperate prayer. "Oh, dear God, what have I done?"

"Actually, it means Lillian has married her stepbrother." And that was the only consolation in this whole family-tree catastrophe.

Frederick's eyes snapped open. "But how can that be? You and Sara—"

"Had no children of our own. Sara was in love with my best friend, a man named Neal Farrell. He was killed in a riding accident before they could marry. When she learned she was with child, she came to me, terrified of what her father would do when he found out."

Frederick thought for a moment. "So you married her and raised Lillian as your own."

Marcus nodded. "No one ever knew Lillian wasn't mine except me and Sara. We both thought keeping it from Lillian was the right thing to do."

"So Lillian didn't marry her half brother," Frederick said, now sounding like a captive set free. "Why, Marcus, this is wonderful!"

With a raised brow, Marcus turned to his brother-in-law. "Really? How do you think Lillian is going to react when I tell her I'm not really her father? That I've lived a lie for the past twenty years?"

Frederick thought for a moment. "I think once she gets over the initial shock, she'll be grateful she and Ethan can live as husband and wife without breaking God's law."

Perhaps, Marcus reasoned in his mind. But he was about to destroy the sacred trust that had always existed between him and his daughter. She'd once looked at him as though he'd helped God hang the sun and moon. Would she ever look at him that way again?

Then there were Ethan and Emily. How would they respond to Marcus?

"Tell me, Frederick. Tell me about my twins."

A fond smile tugged at the corner of the minister's lips.

"Ethan is a mountain of strength. He's smart and proud—all the things you would want your son to be. And he loves Lillian with all his heart.

"Emily has a gift of administering to the sick with medicinal herbs. She's every bit as talented and lovely as her mother. Unfortunately, she lost her husband while her children were still in her womb. He was murdered by two gold miners trespassing on his land."

While Frederick continued to speak, contrasting emotions tangled inside Marcus. So much gratefulness that his children had turned out to be fine people. So much sorrow that he'd missed being a part of their childhood. So much anger at the pain that had been forced upon the Cherokee people by the hand of his very own race.

So much anticipation over what lay ahead.

For the first time in his life, Marcus Gunter faced the future with the gripping fear of uncertainty. How was he going to tell the daughter he'd raised as his own for two decades that he wasn't really her father? How was he going to meet the grown children he didn't know?

Slowly, he closed his eyes and wet his parched lips. How was he going to face Mary Snowbird Walker again?

⁂

Four days later, Marcus, seated astride his chestnut gelding, followed Frederick and his mount into a narrow ravine leading to what Snowbird had referred to in her letter as the Blue Haven. Marcus could see why the Cherokee had chosen the obscure valley for their place of refuge. During their journey, he and Frederick had wrestled terrain no man would challenge without good reason. Abundant trees and foliage hid the entrance. The intimidating Appalachian Mountains protected the dale on all sides. Marcus felt like he was riding into a wilderness, being swallowed up by the vast land that, he suspected, had never been touched by man until recently.

How had his daughter survived it? She had grown up on a Virginia plantation with servants to see to her every need. Even though she had somehow remained unspoiled, she had never been exposed to such crude conditions as these. She'd never been forced to sleep on the ground, wash her clothes in a stream, or bathe in a river.

When the passageway widened, sweat dampened Marcus's palms. As a soldier, he'd faced his share of battles. But nothing could prepare him for what lay ahead: a grown son and daughter he did not know, the woman he'd raised who was about to find out he wasn't her father, and the woman who'd once held his heart in the palm of her hand.

Finally, the ravine fanned away, opening up to a primitive village nestled on a recently cleared parcel of land. Thatch-roofed huts with walls of buckskin, canvas, or various other heavy materials lined the outer rim of the clearing. Busy coppery-skinned Cherokees of all ages dotted the village. Some worked at stretching an animal skin out to dry; some prepared food over a small fire; others tended a bountiful vegetable garden. One by one, they noticed him and Frederick.

In order not to alarm the Indians, Marcus had worn civilian clothes instead of his uniform. A federal soldier meant certain captivity and a devastating journey west for the Cherokee. Still, the natives approached with caution, greeting Frederick with a solemn nod and Marcus with wary suspicion.

But Marcus wasn't concerned with the Indians' acceptance or rejection of him. His sole focus was on finding his daughter.

"Papa!"

He caught the glint of her light blond hair glistening in the morning sunlight at the same time she called his name. Breaking away from the crowd, she ran toward him, waving and calling out to him again.

He threw his right leg over the gelding's neck and slid off the saddle without taking the time to rein in his horse. Racing to meet her halfway, he wrapped her in a crushing hug.

"Lillian," he said, his voice husky with relief. "Thanks to God, you're all right. I've been out of my mind with worry."

Drawing back, his daughter looked up at him. "I'm sorry, Papa. I couldn't let you know what happened. Too much was at risk."

He framed her face with his hands, assuring himself she was there, alive and unharmed. The sun had turned her fair skin golden, and her cheeks held a rosy glow he'd never noticed before. But in the depths of her forest green eyes, a profound sadness lingered.

"You could have at least sent word you were all right," he gently scolded.

Her mouth dropped open as though she suddenly remembered something of great importance. "How did you find out where I was? Did Uncle Frederick tell you?"

Marcus told her about Snowbird's letter.

When he finished, she timidly wet her lips. "Then you know I'm married. . . ."

The unspoken words "to my half brother" hung heavy between them. Marcus couldn't put off telling her the truth much longer. It might destroy the familiar bond that had existed between him and Lillian, but at least it would release her to live as a wife to the man she'd pledged to love until death. At least it would banish the hollowness in her eyes.

"Yes, I know you're married," he said, shifting his gaze to the man standing behind her right shoulder. "And this must be your husband."

Lillian stepped aside, and Marcus, for the first time in his life, faced the stranger who was his son. Glossy, shoulder-length black hair brushed his shoulders. He stood slightly taller and a little broader than Marcus. His skin was a few shades darker, his jaw a bit more square. But his eyes. . .

In her letter, Snowbird had said their son had Marcus's eyes, and he did. They were the exact same shade of blue, neither dark nor light. But where Marcus knew his must be anxious, anticipating, his son's were hard and brimming with acrimony. Even so, such an overwhelming sense of pride gripped Marcus, he could hardly breathe.

This is my son, he thought. *My blood flows through his veins. His flesh is of mine.* Marcus's vision blurred. He squeezed his eyes shut and pinched the bridge of his nose. *Dear Lord, if I can't be his father, then at least let me be his friend.*

Suddenly and without warning, Marcus's awareness heightened, drawing his attention to another place among the crowd. He shifted his gaze slightly to his left, and there she stood in a dress of deep green, her long black hair in a single braid and draped over one shoulder, her chin tilted at a proud angle. A group of Cherokee men surrounded her, boldly protecting her like a fortress wall and daring him to break through. But their silent warning swiftly lost its effectiveness when the piercing eyes and contemptuous faces all faded away except for one.

Her dark beauty fascinated him. She'd been lovely as a fifteen-year-old, but time and life had groomed her into a strikingly beautiful woman. His throat grew dry, and once again, his palms felt sweaty. A smothering hand, it seemed, pressed down upon his chest.

All at once, her brown eyes softened. A latent bond arose and then began to reconnect. A vast canyon carved by years and distance shrank a bit. Then, like a vapor in the wind, the warmth in her gaze vanished, and a harsh shadow fell over her face, severing the tenuous link.

Despite the smothering heat, a chill raced down his body and up his arms, jerking him back to reality. He'd apparently imagined her spirit reaching out to his. After all, twenty-seven years had carved a chasm too deep and too wide for either of them to cross.

three

Snowbird went back to what she had been doing before Marcus's arrival—grinding meal. She preferred the pretense of concentrating on crushing dried kernels in a wooden bowl over showing her anguish at what was transpiring between Marcus, his son, and his daughter. Counting each twist of the smooth stone in her hand gave her something to think about besides her unanticipated weakness.

For a fleeting moment, she had felt sympathy for Marcus and the task that lay ahead of him. She knew from experience that confronting the young couple's agony wasn't easy. Then she had reminded herself Marcus was just as much to blame for Ethan and Lillian's tragedy as she. Perhaps more so. If he hadn't abandoned her twenty-seven years ago, things could have been a lot different.

A surge of anger shot through her, but she ground her teeth, fighting the ire. She didn't like the emotions that memories of Marcus stirred in her. Careless reminiscing pushed her too close to the edge of losing control—and to the resurrection of feelings she had buried long ago.

A droplet of sweat dripped off her nose and splattered on the top of her meal-dusty hand, offering her a welcome distraction. She sat back on her heels and, with her apron, wiped the moisture from her face and neck. Even the shade of an ancient oak offered little reprieve from the scorching June heat. The air draped the valley like a warm blanket in a sweat lodge. Trees, wildflowers, and even the usually thriving evergreens had lost their luster. The community garden flourished only because she and her people carried water to it from the valley lake.

She dropped her apron and looked toward the lake, a body of water hidden by a thick wall of trees and laurel thickets. She knew that was where Ethan had taken Marcus and Lillian to talk. All private conversations took place on the lake's shore, away from the eyes and ears of those not involved in the matter at hand. It was where she had taken Ethan the day she had told him he had unknowingly married his half sister. Where she had broken her son's heart.

Pain clutched Snowbird's chest. Things would never be the same between her and her children. How could they be? She had done the one thing she had always forbidden them to do, the one thing she detested. Lie.

Snowbird swallowed past the ache in her throat and drew in a troubled breath. Had she done the right thing in contacting Marcus? Even though Ethan and Lillian had decided to follow the law of their Bible by living as man and wife but in separate quarters, the young couple had seemed in better spirits since they had learned Lillian was with child a week ago.

Closing her eyes, Snowbird mentally shook her head. She had done the right thing, she reminded herself. Living in the same small village with each other while not being able to express their romantic love, not even in the form of a modest kiss, would eventually destroy the young lovers. Lillian needed her father to take her back to her Virginia plantation where she belonged so she could raise her child in civilization instead of in a desolate mountain village.

Snowbird pursed her lips. Ethan would agree. He was not

a selfish man. Once he thought it through, he would accept that Lillian should give birth to their child in the safety and comfort of her Virginia home. The Cherokee Removal had forced upon his people horrendous living conditions. Ethan would not want Lillian to deliver the babe in the wilderness.

An indefinable sensation prompted Snowbird to open her eyes. When she did, she found Marcus approaching from the direction of the lake, clouds of parched dust swirling around his booted feet. She wanted to grasp the front of her dress, where a spasm of trepidation squeezed her chest. Instead, she curled one hand around the other in her lap and clenched her teeth.

She and Marcus would talk like the two civilized people they were. They would agree amicably on what was best for their children. Of course, there would be pain, heartbreak, and sorrow in the beginning. But eventually, Ethan and Lillian would go on with their lives.

And Snowbird would never have to lay eyes on Marcus Gunter again.

She lifted her chin a willful inch, determined not to allow herself to feel guilty for her thoughts. The only solution to Ethan and Lillian's dilemma would not only be best for Snowbird but for the young couple, as well. Any other choice would simply prolong their grief.

As Marcus drew near and she moved to stand, her knee caught the lip of the bowl, spilling over half the cornmeal. She froze, her attention drawn to the food now scattered among the dirt and grass and thoughts about the empty stomachs it could fill. Alarm forced her back to her knees, where she scrambled to scrape the meal and dried kernels back into the wooden vessel.

Strong fingers circled her wrist. "Mary, stop."

She twisted her arm from his grasp and resumed scraping. Her people no longer had fine houses with large kitchens and servants to bring them fresh-baked bread at their every whim. Here in the Blue Haven, food was scarce and hunger a familiar feeling. Wasting provisions, even dirty cornmeal, was not an option.

He captured her wrist again, this time a little more firmly. "Mary, it's ruined. You can't use it." His velvety voice was smooth and calm, his touch steady.

Fury singed the corner of her mind. How could he take their children's tragedy with such composure while she was coming unraveled inside?

She stared at his hand, postponing the moment she'd have to look into his eyes. For when she did, the conflicting emotions churning inside her would erupt and break her into a million tiny pieces.

"Everything is going to be all right."

All right? She swallowed the bitter laugh rising in her chest. How could he say everything was going to be all right when his desertion and her deceit had destroyed their son and his daughter?

Closing her eyes, she forced steadiness into her labored breathing. She had to get through this; had to deal with Ethan and Lillian's future in a calm, rational manner; had to think. But how could she with him holding her arm, making her all too aware he was there in the flesh, after twenty-seven years of absence?

She wet her lips. "Please. . .let go of me." Her throat was so dry. So thick.

He did release her, but the feel of his long fingers around

her wrist lingered like a sizzling brand. Without thinking, she pulled her arm to her chest and tried to rub the sensation away.

"I'm sorry." He reached out to her.

She tensed, drawing her arms closer to her body.

Again, he dropped his hand. "I didn't mean to hurt you."

"You didn't," she quickly countered, letting her hands fall to her lap. Still, she couldn't look at him.

"Mary, there's something I need to tell you."

Indignation won the battle against all other emotions chipping away at her fragile control. Through clenched teeth, she managed to say, "My. . .name. . .is not. . .Mary."

"Snowbird," he softly corrected.

Finally, she looked up at him, into eyes as blue as sapphire and a gaze as penetrating and crippling to her defenses as a rattler's bite. Scrambling up, she hugged herself and turned away.

She felt warmth flowing from his body as he stepped up close behind her.

"Ethan and Lillian are not related."

Rage snapped her last thread of control. Spinning around, she slapped him. "How dare you insinuate Ethan is not your son?"

He just stood there, seemingly void of all emotion and unaffected by her reaction, which only infuriated her more. Grasped by a vengeful monster she couldn't control, she raised her hand again, but his snapped up and clamped her wrist before she could deliver the second blow.

"Don't," he warned in a low, unwavering voice. "There are a dozen Cherokee men across the camp waiting for an excuse to string me up. I don't want to give them one by having to restrain you."

She jerked her arm away and stepped back. Chest heaving, she curled her fists at her sides. "Ethan is your son."

"I know, but Lillian is not my daughter."

Stunned, she could only stare at him. He was crazy, she decided. Apparently five days of riding in the torturous sun had robbed him of his sound mind.

"She is the daughter of the man who was my best friend, Neal Farrell," he added, then paused, as though knowing she needed time to grasp what he was saying. "He died before he knew her mother was expecting her. I married Sara to save her and the unborn child from shame."

Snowbird blinked, once, slowly. A single ray of enlightenment needled through her blind fury. "Then. . .Ethan and Lillian. . ."

"Are not related."

For one dazzling moment, her body seemed suspended somewhere between heaven and earth. Then a wave of intense heat flushed her face, rushed down her body, and washed away her last shred of strength.

❧

Snowbird fell like a doe struck down by a hunter's bullet. One minute she was standing, looking at Marcus as if he'd lost his mind, and in the next instant, she lay in a crumpled heap at his feet. He didn't have time to react.

He dropped to his knees beside her, only vaguely aware of the spilt corn kernels biting into his legs. Slipping one hand beneath her head, he caressed her cheek with the other. "Mary, can you hear me?"

She was pale as a lily and clammy. The skin around her mouth was milky white, and a thin strand of her dark hair clung to her damp cheek.

Dark fear swept through him. What had he done to her? He'd thought she'd be glad to hear Ethan and Lillian were not related. At the very least, relieved. The last reaction he'd expected was that she'd pass out.

"Take your hands off her!"

The angry male voice came from above. Before Marcus could look up, a razor-sharp pain shot through his chin and exploded in his temples. His head snapped back. He wobbled but somehow remained upright in his kneeling position.

Training and instinct determined if Marcus would retaliate or wait. Striking back at the young Cherokee man who'd hit him would not meet the immediate need, which was seeing to Snowbird's welfare. And the young man who'd hit him, along with the greater population of the village gathering around her, looked like they were capable of causing him further injury.

"Mother? Can you hear me?" The young man now kneeling at Snowbird's opposite side cradled her in much the same way Marcus had. A young woman dropped to her knees at Snowbird's head and began caressing her cheek.

The Cherokee's reference to Snowbird as his mother registered somewhere in a remote corner of Marcus's mind, but concern for her shrouded the significance in the exchange.

Marcus saw the flicker of her eyes beneath the chalky skin of her eyelids and knew she was regaining consciousness. The bunched muscles between his shoulders began to relax.

Finally her eyes fluttered open, and for a moment, she looked up at the young man with an expression clouded with question and bewilderment. Raising a hand, she touched his face. "Billy?" she asked as though wondering how he had gotten there.

"Yes, Mother. It's Billy."

"Where's Marcus?"

"Here," Marcus answered before anyone else could and leaned forward so she could see him.

With a look of awe that touched a place deep inside Marcus, she reached over and brushed his face with her hand, then slid her exploring fingertips, branded by years of hard labor, to his lips. Her beseeching stroke rocked him to his core, filling him with a desire to draw her hand closer and kiss her palm. Mindful of the critical glares shooting his way, he drew her hand down instead and cocooned it between both of his.

"You really are here." Wonderment and disbelief threaded her tone.

"Yes, M—Snowbird, I'm here." He caressed the back of her hand with his thumb.

"Is it true? That Ethan and Lillian are not related?"

He smiled. "Yes, it's true. Lillian is my adopted daughter. We don't share the same blood."

Snowbird closed her eyes as if she were offering up a silent prayer of thanksgiving. A tear slipped from the outer corner of her eye and trickled across the side of her temple.

A wave of protective emotions crashed into Marcus's chest. He had never seen Snowbird cry before, not even the morning he had left to join the army.

"I'd like to sit up, please."

Marcus and Billy leaned forward at the same time to help Snowbird sit, bumping heads. Marcus glanced up into the proud and determined eyes of the young Cherokee.

"I'll help my mother stand," he said.

The silent message in Billy's words was clear. Marcus was

the intruder here. He had no rights, no claims among the Cherokee people or to the woman whose hand he held.

Relenting, Marcus rocked back on his heels and stood. He watched as Snowbird rose, ready to offer help should she waver. But the lad was both attentive and possessive, making sure no aid was needed from the outsider. After she was on her feet, he continued to steady her with an arm around her waist.

Shifting to face Marcus, she said, "I imagine you would like to meet the rest of your family."

Marcus nodded. He did want to meet the rest of his family: a daughter and two grandchildren.

Snowbird's gaze remained steady on him, even as she called, "Emily!"

The young woman who had helped Billy attend Snowbird stepped forward. Two dark-haired children, a boy and a girl around the age of six, walked beside her, clinging to her skirt. She was petite with dark hair and eyes like her mother and was every bit as lovely, but her skin was fair, like his.

Snowbird waited until her daughter stopped beside her. "This is Emily, Ethan's twin sister. And these two little fawns"—she looked down with affection at the boy and girl peering out from behind the folds of their mother's dress— "are Jed and Julie."

He couldn't take his eyes off her, this woman who was his daughter. A web of tangled emotions—pride, joy, wonder, amazement—clogged his throat. The same feelings he'd experienced when he'd first faced Ethan. Marcus swallowed. How could he have been a part of something so perfect, so wonderful?

Reaching up with her right hand, Emily tucked her hair

behind her left ear, a gesture that indicated she was restless with his hesitation.

He tipped his head forward. "Emily."

Resting a protective hand on each child, she lifted her chin an aloof inch. "Mr. Gunter," she returned. "Or do you prefer Colonel?"

I prefer Papa, he wanted to say but knew from the stubborn set of her jaw and the distance in her eyes that the request would be spurned. "Most call me Colonel, but whatever you feel comfortable with is fine."

She studied him a moment in contemplation. "Colonel," she finally decided.

He wanted to reach out to her, pull her to his chest, and tell her how sorry he was for all he'd missed: her childhood, giving her away at her wedding, being there to comfort her when she lost her husband, being present when his grandchildren came into the world. But the cold reserve in her expression told him if he tried to approach her with even the smallest degree of affection, he'd meet with rejection.

Turning his attention to his grandchildren, he crouched. He turned first to Julie. With her huge black eyes, she studied him curiously. In the crook of one arm, she cradled a cornhusk doll.

Marcus offered her a warm smile. "Hello, Julie. I'm pleased to meet you."

A quick grin brought a sparkle to her black eyes and dimpled her round cheeks. But she remained silent and half tucked away behind her mother's skirt.

Not wanting to upset the already precarious atmosphere, Marcus shifted his attention to Jed, where he was once again met with distrust.

"Hello, Jed."

Jed sidled up even closer to his mother. The knuckles of his small hand clutching the faded material of his mother's dress turned white. Marcus merely nodded and stood.

"I'm sure you and Frederick are tired and hungry," Snowbird said. "Emily and I will prepare you a meal; then you may rest."

"I'll do it, Mother," Emily injected. "You are the one in need of rest."

Emily's comment made it clear to Marcus she would accommodate him only out of concern and respect for her mother, not out of any sense of hospitality she felt toward him.

"Don't bother," he said. "I have provisions left from the trail."

"It's no bother," Snowbird spoke up, her voice soft but firm with authority. "Emily, you will prepare your father a meal."

Without a word, Emily pivoted and disappeared through a small opening the Cherokee made for her retreat. Her two children followed close behind her.

Billy urged Snowbird to do the same. "Come, Mother. I'll take you to your shelter."

Mother. The word needled its way to the front of Marcus's mind. Snowbird had a third child—by another man. Something swift and hard hit Marcus in the chest. Why hadn't Frederick mentioned the boy to Marcus during their journey to the Indian village? And where was Billy's father?

With a few more distrustful glances and a couple of low harrumphs, the Cherokee shuffled away. One man remained facing Marcus. Frederick.

"You didn't tell me Snowbird is married." Marcus was unable to keep the sting of accusation out of his voice.

"She's not."

Confusion marred Marcus's brow. "Where is Billy's father?" he wanted to know.

Thinking, Frederick pursed his wrinkled lips and pocketed his aged fists. "I think Snowbird needs to be the one to talk to you about that."

four

Marcus couldn't get out of his mind the image of Snowbird scraping the spilled corn up off the ground. The alarm on her face when she realized she'd tipped over the bowl, the desperation in each stroke of her hand as she scrambled to save the ruined meal had plagued him all day and followed him into the gloaming hours, when he and Frederick joined Snowbird and her family for the evening meal.

The food was well prepared and delicious, but portions taken from the bowls passed around the blanket on which they sat were modest. No one asked for seconds—not even the children.

When Marcus handed off the clay soup bowl without taking a serving for himself, Lillian's brow creased with concern. "Are you not feeling well, Papa?"

He looked to his left, where she sat. "Emily fed me so well earlier, I'm simply not hungry."

Puzzlement deepened her frown—for she knew he had a healthy appetite—but then an expression of understanding smoothed her brow. Without asking, she laid a piece of corn bread on his plate. "Here, at least have some bread. I made it."

Marcus felt the curious stares and knew Lillian was looking out for him. To shun the hospitality of the Cherokee would be an insult to them, so he picked up his plate and ate.

When everyone finished their meal, Jed and Julie helped

their mother and Snowbird carry the dishes to a nearby stream to wash up.

The Blue Haven Cherokee worked in incredible unison, each doing whatever needed to be done without being asked. It was as though they all, from the youngest to the oldest, knew their survival depended on the silent code of harmony by which they lived.

Marcus's offers of help were refused, so he and Frederick visited with Snowbird's great-grandfather, the clan's chief, while Lillian and Ethan prepared a place for Marcus and Frederick to sleep.

Clearly, Ethan cherished Lillian and she him. Marcus saw undeniable devotion in every starry look and each tender touch that passed between them.

God, please never let anything—or anyone—come between them. And please, let me never have reason to cause them grief. He never would forget the day he, through his own father's lie, lost Snowbird. The crippling devastation and searing agony had burned a hole in his soul that had never quite healed.

Marcus would rather die than cause another that kind of pain.

Knowing sleep would come slowly that night, Marcus excused himself for a walk as everyone else settled in for the evening, then made his way to the lake by the light of a half-moon, stopping for a time beside the water's edge. The melodious sound of night creatures, small animals scurrying through the bushes, and the underlying silence surrounded him. The dewy air brushed his skin with a whisper of coolness. The sparkling reflection of moon and stars on the placid pool shimmered like diamonds sprinkled across black silk.

Still waters. The Bible promised that beside them one would find peace and tranquility, rest and restoration. But tonight, all thoughts of serenity escaped Marcus. He faced a colossal problem and needed to figure out what to do about it—how to help the Blue Haven Cherokee without deserting his duties as an officer of the U.S. Army.

He found a grassy place a few feet from the lake's shore and sat down to think.

For the fourth time that night, Snowbird lifted the buckskin doorway of the thatched-roof shelter she shared with Emily and her children and ducked outside. The moon casting dwarfish shadows across the camp told her the midnight hour was fast approaching.

Where was Marcus?

She had seen him slip away from the village earlier, but that had been hours ago. Even though she couldn't see inside the shelter where he was to lodge, she knew he had not yet returned. The horses would have alerted her to his arrival.

Her skin tingled, and she pulled her thin shawl tighter around her shoulders. Although the summer days in the Blue Haven were hot and suffocating, a nipping chill attacked the Appalachian Mountains after sunset.

Crossing her arms, she strolled toward the end of the village nearest the hidden lake. Several of the horses, including Marcus's and Frederick's mounts, raised their heads, quirked their ears, and shuffled a bit. One neighed softly.

Ethan, born with the alertness of a mountain lion, poked his head outside his and Lillian's shelter. His makeshift home was in the direction Snowbird was walking, so he slipped the rest of the way outside and met her halfway.

Stepping up to her, he rested his hands on her upper arms. "What's wrong, Mother?"

"Marcus left the camp some time ago. Did he tell you where he was going?"

"To take a walk down by the lake." Ethan glanced up and studied the sky. "But that was right after nightfall. He should have come back by now."

"I know." Snowbird shifted her gaze toward the wall of trees beyond Ethan's shoulder. "He doesn't know the area. I was beginning to worry he'd taken a fall or crossed paths with the mountain lion that attacked one of our calves the other night."

"I'll go look for him," Ethan said and ducked back inside his shelter for his moccasins.

"We'll both go," Snowbird said when he returned, and she stepped into the wooded shadows before he could protest.

Since Marcus had told Ethan he was going to the lake, that's where they started looking. And that's where they found him. Snowbird stopped short of stepping beyond the shadows. Ethan paused beside her.

Marcus sat staring out over the water like a man who carried a grievous burden on his shoulders.

Relief at finding him flooded Snowbird, as did a wellspring of compassion for the weary man sitting beside the lakeshore. Straightening her spine, she summoned her defenses and reminded herself he had taken her innocence and then turned his back on her. He did not deserve her compassion. Whatever it was that plagued him—guilt when he looked into the faces of his grown children, regret for missing their childhood—he'd brought on himself.

"Looks like he could use someone to talk to," Ethan

whispered near her ear.

"I wouldn't bother, if I were you," she whispered back. "If he wants to sit out here in the cool of the night when he could be underneath a warm blanket, let him do so alone." She turned to go.

Ethan stopped her with a hand on her upper arm. "I wasn't talking about myself."

Snowbird's chin dropped. "Surely you don't think I'm going to entertain that man at this hour?"

"Who's there?" came Marcus's voice, curious but calm.

They both turned to look in Marcus's direction. He now stood, looking toward the shadows.

"Now look what you've done," Snowbird scolded under her breath. "You can stay if you like. I'm going back to the village."

She tried to leave, but her son's hold was firm and unyielding.

"Listen to me, Mother. There are things you and he need to talk about. Things he told Lillian and me this morning."

Snowbird didn't want to hear anything Marcus had to say. "If it's so important, why can't you tell me in the morning?"

"Snowbird?"

Snowbird refused to look Marcus's way, but the sound of his voice revealed he'd stepped closer.

"Go on, Mother," Ethan urged. "Let him tell you what really happened all those years ago."

She knew what happened twenty-seven years ago. He used her and then discarded her like a spoiled child does a soiled doll. She opened her mouth to protest again, but Ethan had already released her and disappeared into the shadows.

She took a few seconds to collect her thoughts. What should she do? Go. . .or stay?

A twig snapped. Gasping, she whipped around. Two strong hands clasped her upper arms exactly where Ethan's had. Only these hands instantly heated her skin in spite of two protective layers of clothing. Like avoiding a whipping flame, she leaped back, forcing him to release her.

"I'm sorry," he said. "I didn't mean to frighten you."

"You didn't," she replied a bit too quickly. At least the sound of the twig snapping had not frightened her. She was used to little inconspicuous sounds like a twig snapping, small animals scrambling for cover, the abrupt halt of birdsong. No, his approach had not alarmed her, but his near presence scared her to death. Not because of anything he might do, but because she was afraid of herself and her reaction to him. Where had all her hard-won defenses gone?

He cast a searching glance past her shoulder. "Wasn't that Ethan I heard with you? Where did he go?"

"Back to the camp. I suppose I should be going also."

"What are you doing out here so late?" he asked before she could make her retreat.

"I. . .we. . .grew concerned for your safety when you didn't return to camp."

"I didn't mean to worry anyone. I guess time just slipped away."

An awkward silence fell between them like when two strangers searched for conversation. And while she wanted to leave, something deep inside convinced her she should stay. In the darkness, he was a mere shadow, but she felt his gaze upon her, trying to read her mind the same way she was trying to read his. Was he also left wondering?

"Snowbird, we need to talk."

She released a slow sigh. She supposed they did need to

talk about family matters and such. After all, they shared both children and grandchildren. And in judging Marcus's reaction to his newfound family—the way he interacted with Ethan, the way he looked with longing and adoration at his grandchildren, his devotion to his adopted daughter—she knew he would not stay away forever as Snowbird had initially hoped.

"All right," she said.

"Let's go sit beside the lake." The silhouette of his hand swept out, bidding her to precede him. She did so, and when she stepped into the moonlight, she felt exposed, as if he could see her nerves jumping and hear her heart pounding.

Relax. He just wants to talk. No harm in that.

At his suggestion, they stopped near where he had been. She sank down in the dew-kissed grass, crisscrossing her legs beneath her full skirt. He looped his arms around his bent knees.

Since he was the one wanting to talk, she waited for him to start.

"Snowbird, do you have anyone to take care of you?"

She angled her head to look at him, but refusing to meet her gaze, he continued to stare out over the water.

"Of course I do," she said. "We all take care of each other here."

"That's not what I mean." A moment passed; then he finally looked her way. "No one will tell me where or who Billy's father is."

A sick feeling of dread curled in the pit of her stomach. She had not anticipated her youngest son's parentage to be the topic of their conversation. What should she tell Marcus? That Billy's father was none of his concern? Instinctively, she knew that response would never satisfy Marcus. If he didn't get the truth from her, he'd keep seeking until he got it from someone else.

It was she who cast her eyes toward the lake this time. Taking a deep, bracing breath, she said, "No one will tell you about Billy's father because no one can. . . . Not even me."

The silence that fell between them was so thick and heavy, Snowbird thought she could hear the stars breathe.

"I was attacked by three drunken white men. They. . .forced themselves upon me. They were operating an illegal still in the foothills near our village. I came upon them one morning while I was out gathering herbs. Unfortunately, Ethan was with me and witnessed the. . .assault." Her voice lacked emotion, she knew. But the only way she could repeat the story was to detach her feelings from the horrid incident, pretend she was talking about a stranger.

For a long time, Marcus said nothing, which didn't surprise her. Silence was how everyone reacted to the knowledge of her tragedy.

"I'm sorry, Snowbird," he finally said, his voice raspy and ringing with sympathy.

But she didn't want sympathy, his or anyone else's. She tipped her chin a stubborn inch. "I survived."

Did you really? a defiant voice seemed to whisper inside her head. *If you survived, then why did you stop living on that day?* "And I have Billy," she added, trying to silence the voice in her mind. "He's a good boy, and I'm grateful I have him."

❧

Think, Marcus told himself. *Think beyond the rage and anger building inside you. Rage at what happened to her. Rage that she suffered so. Rage that you were not there to protect her. Rage at your father and the lie he told twenty-seven years ago.*

Marcus breathed deep, past the ache in his throat and the tightness in his chest. Picking up a thick twig, he grasped it in both hands. *Why, Lord, why? Why did this have to happen to her? Why was I not there to help her through it. . .or prevent it? Why?*

The twig snapped, jerking him back into the present and reminding him of his need to talk to Snowbird. With great effort, he swallowed. "I want to help, Snowbird. I'd like to take you and our families to my home in Virginia. There's plenty of room," he went on before she could protest, because he knew she would. "You, your great-grandfather, Billy, our children and grandchildren need never live in fear again."

Slowly she turned her head and glared at him as if he'd gone daft. "Marcus, when the government found out we were there, they would remove us anyway. Just like they will if they find out we are here."

Marcus realized then what a risk Snowbird had taken by writing him that letter two weeks ago. She had not known him for years. How could she know whether he would reveal her people's whereabouts or come riding into the valley with a troop of soldiers to round up the entire village and take them to a filthy, disease-infested stockade?

She couldn't have. She had made a choice and risked freedom and the scorn of her people for the sake of their son. . .and his daughter.

An overwhelming sense of gratitude swept through Marcus. He wanted so much to reach over and take her hand, tell her everything would be all right, that he would take care of her for the rest of their lives. But he knew better. She'd reject him, just as she was going to reject his offer of help. Still, he tried.

"No one need know where you and your family are, Snowbird, whether it's here in the Blue Haven or in Virginia. I'll do everything within my power to see that doesn't happen."

Her shoulders relaxed with visible relief. "Thank you, Marcus. You have no idea what that means to me."

No, he didn't. He'd never had to flee his home or hide from an unjust government. He could only imagine. "If I could undo what the government has done to you and your people, I would. But I can't. I can only offer you and those closest to you a place to live where you'll never have to worry where your next meal is going to come from or whether or not you'll have to sleep in snow or rain."

She studied the lake as though contemplating her choices. "I appreciate your offer, Marcus, and your concern. Whatever the children want to do is all right with me. But I have a duty to my people. My place is with them, just like your place, as a soldier of the United States Army, is with your regiment."

Her answer was what he'd expected. Her people looked to her for guidance and leadership, and in the few hours since he'd ridden into the valley, he'd witnessed her loyalty to them, which didn't surprise him. Her words implied there was nothing left between them. They both were bound to different causes, obligations that put them on opposite sides of a battlefield neither of them knew how to cross.

He filtered a relenting sigh. He knew not to press her. While he wished she would accept his offer, he also respected and understood her patriotism. He'd make the same proposition to Ethan and Emily as he had Snowbird. But Marcus already knew what their answer would be. Like their mother, their loyalty was with the Cherokee people in the village. As for Lillian, hers was to her husband, as it should be. "I'll send food and supplies by Frederick."

She swallowed hard. "Thank you."

Marcus knew her acceptance of his second offer had been hard, the actions of a proud woman doing what was best for a desperate people.

He raked a weary hand over his face. They'd had something so special once. Did the ache and disappointment inside him come from hoping a remnant of that something still existed? Would telling her why he didn't come after her all those years ago make a difference? Did he want it to? Or was what he was feeling right now—a desire to hold her, a need to erase all her pain—just a reaction to an extremely emotional day?

He didn't know the answers to any of the questions swirling around his mind. He just knew that he, a usually sensible, pragmatic man, had a stream of emotions twisting inside his chest, crippling his ability to reason.

"I'm going back to the village," she said, penetrating his heavy thoughts.

"One more thing," he said as she started to rise.

She paused for a heartbeat, then settled back down on the grass and waited.

"I thought you were dead, Snowbird."

She blinked twice, then wet her lips. They glistened in the moonlight. Her shoulders quivered, and she clasped her hands tightly in her lap. "Wh–what do you mean?" Her voice sounded small and tremulous.

Anyone could look at her and see trials over the forced removal and concern over her people's welfare had taken a tremendous toll on her. He didn't want her to pass out again.

He shifted to kneel in front of her, bracing her with his

hands on her upper arms, grateful when she didn't pull away. "I thought you were dead."

Like a stone statue, silent and still, she stared at him. Even as her eyes filled, she did not move. Not even to breathe.

Marcus's chest swelled with something he'd thought dead and buried long ago.

He caressed her cool cheek with the backs of his fingers. "I came back for you, Snowbird, just like I promised. But my father told me you had died of the fever. He even showed me a grave he'd apparently prepared to serve his selfish purposes." He waited, letting her absorb his words before adding, "I didn't know you were alive until I received your letter five days ago."

Words throbbed inside him, fighting to escape, until he thought he would explode. Something told him if he didn't say them now, opportunity would pass him by and he might never get the chance or the courage again. "I really did love you then, Snowbird. I think I still do."

He waited for what seemed like an eternity for her to say or do something. Instead, she sat motionless, staring at him as if he were a creature and she was afraid to move for fear he might consume her.

A tear slipped from her eye, flowed down her cheek, and spread across his forefinger. That single drop of moisture rocked him to his core. He leaned forward until his lips were a mere breath from hers.

His action seemed to jerk her out of the trance holding her captive. Pushing away, she scrambled up off the ground, swiping one hand across one side of her face and then the other.

Marcus stood more slowly and faced her.

Something akin to anger tensed her jaw and drew her lips into a thin line. "It is very late. If you intend to ride out tomorrow, you need to get some rest. Good night, Marcus." With that, she turned and marched away.

"Wait," he said, running after her. "I'll walk back with you."

He saw her to the door of her shelter, then went to the one Ethan and Lillian had earlier prepared for him and Frederick. The minister lay softly snoring in peaceful slumber. The moonlight bathed the buckskin walls, casting a golden glow across the humble interior, evoking a false sense of calm. But for Marcus, there was no inner peace, no calmness or tranquility. And he had a feeling there would not be for a very long time. . .if ever again.

He sat down, tugging at the laces of his boots. He was grateful he'd found his daughter and was able to give her back her marriage. He felt especially blessed he'd met the two children and grandchildren he'd learned of just a few short days ago. But he'd also found something he didn't expect: that his feelings for Snowbird had not changed.

As he stretched out on his back on a rough woolen blanket, he struggled with guilt. Sara had been a good wife. Faithful and supportive, a wonderful mother to their daughter. Tragic circumstances had thrown them together, and they'd made the best of it. They'd even grown to love each other as husband and wife.

But where he and Sara had shared a spark, he and Snowbird had breathed life into a flame. And tonight, he'd realized he loved her as much as he ever did. Perhaps even more.

Apparently, though, she didn't feel the same.

He folded his arms behind his head, crossed his legs at the ankles, and stared unseeing at the shadowed roof. He hadn't planned to leave tomorrow morning, but obviously Snowbird wanted him to. He would honor that request.

A big fist seemed to press into his stomach, pushing pain up to his throat. The first time he lost her, devastation had crushed him.

Now that he knew she was alive, now that he'd found her, how could he bear to lose her again?

five

Across the village, Snowbird lay on her back, staring up at her shelter's thatched roof. She rested the back of her hand on her forehead but didn't close her eyes. How could she with the wild thoughts shooting like arrows through her head?

Marcus Gunter was crazy, she had decided. How could he possibly think he still loved her after twenty-seven years? They were such different people now than they were then. They lived such different lives.

Narrowing her eyes, she contemplated his tone, his eager touch when he'd told her he loved her down by the river. He had spoken and touched her with such conviction. Even if he still had a small degree of affection for her, how could he know so soon?

The same way you do.

Twisting around to lie on her side, she shushed the voice inside. She adjusted the rolled-up blanket she used for a pillow. Then, drawing up her knees, she crossed her arms in determination. Yes, she had almost responded to Marcus's pledge of love, had almost given in when he started to kiss her.

But she hadn't.

Just in time, she reminded herself she wasn't the naive fifteen-year-old she'd been that last night they'd met in the Spring Place garden. The night she had recklessly succumbed to feelings nature was awakening in her. She was much older now. . .and much wiser. Too wise to become distracted by a romantic fantasy.

But he thought you were dead, her stubborn conscience persisted.

So he did, she begrudgingly admitted to herself. Snowbird had known Marcus's father was prejudiced, driven by bigotry and his so-called Savior. Reverend Gunter thought Jesus came to save one race—the one with fair skin.

For twenty-seven years, she had blamed Marcus for betraying her, when in reality, his father had betrayed them both. A swell of constantly simmering anger arose and shifted direction from son to father.

She no longer had a reason to hold a grudge against Marcus; no longer had a reason to hate him; no longer had a barrier between her heart and feelings she knew lay buried deep inside her, awaiting resurrection.

I can't let that happen, she told herself. Her people depended on her to help see them through the treacherous days ahead. She couldn't allow herself to fall in love with Marcus Gunter again, for her clan's sake, as well as her own.

Snowbird's troubled thoughts finally gave way to a restless slumber, and when she rose the next morning, she found Marcus and Frederick had gone.

🙠

One week later

"Jesus, heal my son."

Snowbird watched and listened in agony as Emily prayed for her child.

The young mother dipped a cloth into a bowl of water, then laid it across Jed's fevered brow.

The six-year-old lay on a blanket that smelled of his sickness, his knees drawn up to his cramping stomach, his small body convulsing with a fevered chill.

A solitary candle sat on a tree-stump table, its amber light throwing ghostlike shadows across the shelter's humble buckskin walls.

Two days ago, Jed had been stricken with a ruthless bout of dysentery and vomiting. Everything Emily, a gifted medicine woman, had tried had failed. She had only one more option—wild cherry bark tea. But the wild cherry tree did not grow in the valley.

"About a half mile outside the valley, there is an orchard of wild cherry trees."

Snowbird's head snapped up. "But—"

Just as sharply, Emily raised her head and looked at Snowbird with determination. "If I leave now, I can be back by sunrise."

Snowbird studied Emily with both trepidation and understanding. Jed was her son. She would do whatever it took to save his life, even leave the safety of the valley and venture out into an area where soldiers might be scavenging the woods in search of Indians who were dodging the forced removal.

She laid a hand on her daughter's arm. "Let me go instead."

Emily shook her head. "No. It could take you too long to find the grove. I know exactly where it is."

"Then take Ethan with you."

"There's no need for both of us to take that risk."

"Your brother has the instincts of an eagle. He can sense danger long before it arrives."

Emily chewed her lower lip in contemplation for a moment, then nodded.

Snowbird's shoulders slumped with relief.

With a desperate plea in her eyes, Emily met and held Snowbird's gaze. "Mother, promise you'll pray for Jed while I'm gone."

Snowbird opened her mouth to respond, but her voice failed. She had stopped praying seventeen years ago—the day Billy was conceived. She'd stopped believing in divine deliverance and started questioning God's existence.

If He really did exist, why would He listen to her now after so many years of silence? Why would He even care what troubled her?

"Please, Mother. For Jed."

Resistance fleeing in the face of her daughter's plea, Snowbird nodded. Her prayers might not do any good, but surely they could do no harm.

As Emily slipped from the shelter, Snowbird laid a trembling hand on the side of her sick grandson's parched face, bowed her head, and closed her eyes.

"Lord, I may not be deserving of Your favor, but Jed is only six years old. He loves You. He believes in You. Please, please heal him."

She remained with her head bowed and her hand on Jed's face a few minutes longer. She felt no peace, no comfort. It was as if she had a deep, dark hole carved inside her that needed filling.

She went back to bathing Jed with cool water and noticed his chills were beginning to subside and sweat was beading his forehead.

Not many minutes later, Ethan stuck his head inside the shelter. "How is he doing?"

Looking up, Snowbird blinked in surprise. "Perhaps a little better. Where's Emily?"

Befuddlement pinched Ethan's forehead. "I thought she was here with you and Jed."

A shiver of fear prickled Snowbird's skin. "She went outside the valley to get some wild cherry tree bark to make some tea for Jed. She was supposed to awaken you and take you with her."

Keeping his dark, serious gaze on Snowbird's face, he stepped inside the tent. As he crouched down before her at Jed's opposite side, an impending sense of doom rolled into the shelter like a heavy mist. Ethan had a foretelling awareness when it came to his twin. He always knew when she was in trouble. The look on his face told Snowbird he sensed something had gone awry with his sibling now.

Snowbird's breath froze in her throat.

"I was awakened, but not by Emily," Ethan said, his brow wrinkled in contemplation. "Perhaps it *was* her. I thought I heard something. . .or someone. . .walking past my shelter."

❧

Ethan and Billy had been gone searching for Emily less than two hours before they returned. When Snowbird heard the horses approach, she left Jed with Lillian and ran to meet them. From the grim looks on their faces, she knew the news was not good.

Swinging his leg over his mount's neck, Ethan dismounted as the horse skidded to a stop. He captured Snowbird's upper arms. "She's been taken by federal soldiers."

"No." Snowbird's knees began to buckle. She grasped the front of Ethan's shirt to keep from falling.

Ethan's grip on her arms tightened. "We'll get her back, Mother."

"What about the pact?" John Waters, a young husband and father asked.

While planning their escape to the mountains, clan members had made a pact that they would not allow the capture of one to jeopardize the safety and freedom of other clan members.

Ethan cast an understanding glance John's way. "We're not asking anyone else to join the search, John Waters. Emily is Billy's and my sister. She's our responsibility."

Looking back at his mother, he added, "We'll send word to Frederick. . .and my father. They can help."

A thread of strength returned to Snowbird's limbs. "Yes. Go to Marcus. He will help." After all, Emily was his daughter. Snowbird had seen the way he had looked at her when he was in the valley. He adored her even though she had shunned him.

Yes, Snowbird was confident Marcus Gunter would find a way to gain Emily's release from the U.S. government.

❧

On the day his mother was captured, Jed miraculously began to heal. So swift was his progress that, in three days, he showed an interest in playing with his friends and torturing his twin sister.

Yet his mother wasn't there to see his recovery. Unless those searching for Emily had found her, she didn't know if Jed was dead or alive.

Why?

Often, Snowbird looked toward the heavens and pondered the question. Why had the God Emily so vehemently believed in allowed her to be captured, separated from her children? Why hadn't Snowbird herself been more adamant about going in search of the cherry bark?

Why? Why? Why?

No matter how many times Snowbird asked that question, no one answered. Of course, Snowbird couldn't blame God. She'd done nothing to merit His mercy. Perhaps her punishment was in not knowing where or how her daughter was. Snowbird's children were close to her. She had always known where they were and whether or not they were safe.

Not knowing was torture for her, although for the sake of her grandchildren, she somehow managed to stay focused on life in the valley.

When they asked about their mother, Snowbird was honest about her daughter's capture, explaining to the twins that their uncles had gone to look for her. That was all the anxious children needed to hear. In their eyes, Uncle Ethan and Uncle Billy could do anything. Jed and Julie were confident that their mother would be back soon.

Oh, to see the world through the eyes of a child, Snowbird thought.

But even a child's resilience had its breaking point. After a week without their mother, Jed and Julie began to argue with each other and with Snowbird. They also whined a lot and shadowed Snowbird's every step.

Snowbird constantly told herself that it wouldn't last forever. Ethan and Billy would find Emily, bring her home, and their lives would return to normal.

ಭ

Three weeks later

"Riders coming in!" a young Cherokee man called from across the village.

Snowbird looked up from the task of teaching the twins how to make single-seam ankle moccasins to see four riders trudging into the valley. Immediately she recognized the mounts as those belonging to Ethan, Billy, Marcus, and Frederick. Heart pounding, she laid aside the moccasins. At the same time, Jed and Julie jumped up and ran toward their uncles.

Snowbird grasped the front of her blouse and rose more slowly. Before moving forward, she searched for her daughter. She wasn't riding in front of one of the men. Was she riding behind one of them, her small frame hidden by a bigger one?

As Jed and Julie approached their uncles, Ethan and Billy dismounted. Ethan picked up Jed, and Billy picked up Julie. The two men turned and walked away from the slowly gathering crowd. Frederick dismounted and followed behind Ethan and Billy.

Marcus, who had spotted Snowbird, continued to ride forward. The closer he got, the harder Snowbird's heart thundered inside her chest. Her mouth dried. Her stomach tensed. Her grip tightened on the front of her dress.

Emily was not with him.

Snowbird could not breathe, could not move.

Reining in his chestnut gelding several feet away from her, he dismounted. Their gazes locked. He reached into his saddlebag and pulled out Emily's bloodstained medicine pouch. Eyes rimmed with raw grief, he gingerly stepped up to her. "We found this," he said in a voice raspy with pain, "hanging on a cross. . .marking a grave."

Slowly shaking her head in denial, Snowbird inched back on trembling legs. "No," she croaked. "No, no, no." Lifting her skirt, she spun and ran.

"Snowbird, wait!"

Marcus captured her elbow and turned her around, bracing her by holding on to her upper arms.

In a blind rage, she beat his chest with her fists. "No! It isn't true! It isn't true! She's not dead! She's not dead!"

"Snowbird, I'm sorry." He pulled her close, wrapping his strong arms around her until she could fight no more. Sliding his palm from the crown of her head to the middle of her back, he gently began to rock her from side to side. "I'm sorry. I'm so, so sorry." He kissed the top of her head, then rested his cheek against her hair.

An agonizing sob tore through Snowbird's body, and she went limp. Her only support was the protective arms embracing her.

And while he held Snowbird's shuddering body, Marcus cried in silence.

six

The first light of morning crept through a crack in the door flap of Snowbird's shelter. This night, like the other six since she'd learned of her daughter's death, had passed in fitful slumber. Even though Ethan and Lillian had insisted on keeping Jed and Julie the evening before, sleep had eluded Snowbird.

The ill effects of heartbreak and exhaustion rose to her throat. She pushed up on an elbow and waited for the dizziness and nausea to pass.

Grief was so, so heavy. It would be so easy to succumb to its persistent urging to lie back down. It would be such a release to slip into a dreamless, painless, endless sleep.

Or would it be endless?

The question slipped up on Snowbird from behind, crept into her mind, needled through her thoughts.

Was heaven real? Had Emily gone there? Was there really life after death? How could one know? These were the questions that had plagued Snowbird for the last week.

A rooster's wake-up call penetrated the silence, reminding her people would be stirring soon. If she wanted to slip down to the lake and wash up before breakfast, she'd have to hurry.

She pushed up off her elbow and, with a tired hand, raked back strands of hair loosened from her braid by her night of tossing. She felt so old, as tired and creaky as a woman twice her age. But she had grandchildren—Emily's children—who depended on her now more than ever. A mental picture of Jed and Julie was all she needed to push forward instead of stumble backward, all she needed to find the strength to reach for a clean dress folded in the corner and slip outside her canvas shelter instead of lying back down and giving in to the dark oppression weighing down her body.

As she stepped through the door flap, the coolness of the morning touched her face. She filled her lungs with crisp air, which would soon turn thick and heavy under the merciless heat of drought and sun that had plagued the blue-hued mountains for months. She pressed on toward the lake one weary step at the time. When she entered the thicket separating the camp and lake, she heard the scurry of small creatures running for cover. But she watched the trail border for signs of the larger, quieter mountain lion that had terrorized the livestock recently.

Two steps into the clearing, the sight of a lone figure stopped her. Frederick sat on the bathing rock, a flat boulder at the water's edge. His head was bowed, obviously in prayer.

Feeling like an intruder, Snowbird inched back until a twig snapped beneath her heel. She cringed. How could she have been so careless? As a child, she had been taught to move quietly.

The minister twisted around. "Good morning, Snowbird," he said as though he'd been expecting her. "Why don't you come and sit with me for a while?"

Sit with him? Alone? Would it be proper for a married minister and a single Indian woman with three children out of wedlock? Not much could further tarnish her reputation, but she certainly wouldn't want to blemish his. He was a good man and a loyal friend regarded highly among her people.

"I'm not sure I should," she replied.

Pushing himself up, he stood and faced her. Oddly, he appeared larger than life itself. His white shirt stood out bright and almost glowing against his black suspenders. He had taken off his hat, and his wavy, graying hair touched his collar. His wrinkled face held a gentleness she had never before noticed. Soft blue eyes seemed to look beyond her shabby outward appearance to the dark, cold place deep inside her soul.

Suddenly feeling vulnerable and emotionally exposed, she hugged her clean dress to her chest with one hand and grasped the high collar of her dirty blouse with the other. "Really," she said inching backward, "I should go."

He stepped down off the stone, reaching out a hand to her. "Please, Snowbird, I really would like to talk with you."

A force stronger than her own will halted her retreat. What was it that troubled her heart so? Why did the minister's beckoning seem so hard to resist? Why couldn't she simply turn and walk away?

"Come." Frederick stood before her, hand extended, his penetrating gaze holding hers.

Releasing her dress collar, she slipped her fingers onto his wide, smooth palm.

He led her to the bathing rock where he'd been sitting and assisted her while she sat down. Then he let go of her hand and settled his lean, graceful body beside her. He wrapped his long arms around his folded knees while she laid her clean dress in her lap and arranged her skirts over her crisscrossed legs.

What could he possibly want to talk to her about? Emily? The care of Emily's children? Surely he knew Snowbird was capable of seeing to the needs of her grandchildren. Staring at the still, quiet water, she waited for him to speak.

A few solemn seconds, then, out of the corner of her eye, she saw him turn his head to look at her.

"Snowbird," he said, "how are you doing?"

How was she doing? Should she tell him the truth? That she was devastated? Paralyzed by grief? Suffocated by misery?

"I'll survive," she clipped, not sure where the anger in her voice came from.

He allowed another small silence to pass. "Snowbird, Emily is a Christian. She is with God."

A cautious glimmer of hope tangled with a thin thread of suspicion. Had he realized he'd spoken of Emily in the present tense?

She studied his face to see if she could find something revealing, but his stoic expression told her nothing. "You speak of Emily as though she were still alive."

"For a child of God, death is not the end. It's the sacred passage from this mortal life to life eternal."

Closing her eyes against the sudden sting of tears, she ducked her head and swallowed the overwhelming disappointment. Desperation was such a cruel companion. It made one reach for distant dreams, only to have their hand pass through a shadow.

"Snowbird, I know there's nothing I can say right now to ease your pain. But there is One who can mend your broken heart and heal your wounded spirit."

"I wish I had the faith and the confidence in your God that you do."

"You can, Snowbird. All you have to do is believe in Him, ask Him to come into your heart. Trust Him, and you'll know peace like you've never known before."

Anger singed her heart. Looking up, she met his earnest expression with a rebellious glare. "Trust in Him? My people have been robbed of their land. Those of us who haven't fled to the mountains and been forced to live as fugitives on the run have been dragged out of their homes and locked in pens like swine. The filth is killing them." She swallowed a rising tightness in her throat. "It killed Emily. If God is in control, as you say He is, I don't see Him doing anything to stop the suffering. Tell me, Frederick, how am I supposed to trust in a God like that?"

"Yes, Snowbird, God is in control, but He has also given men a free will and sadly, the hearts of men are evil. They've made this world an evil place. And your believing in Christ will not change their hearts. But it will change yours and how you view the world."

She shook her head in denial. "I don't see how."

"When you look into the eyes of a newborn Cherokee, you will no longer see a child destined for a life of hardship and struggle but a child who, with godly guidance, could someday become one of your people's most effective freedom fighters. Instead of a heart full of hate for those who have wronged you, you will have a heart full of forgiveness and pray they will see the injustice of their evil ways. Instead of looking back and living under the oppression of past tragedies, you will see each day as a new beginning. And inside your heart"— he tapped his chest—"will dwell a peace that surpasses all understanding."

He was daft, she decided. Had to be. How could she pray for those who had robbed her people of their heritage—and her of her daughter?

"What about Emily?" Snowbird's vision blurred. "Do you really think I can pray for the soldiers who took her and caused her death?" She scrubbed the back of her hand across her wet cheek. "Who knows how much she suffered? What they did to her before. . .before. . ." She pressed trembling fingertips against her salty lips. "Oh, Frederick, it isn't fair. It isn't fair!"

The fragile facade she'd clung to for the past seven days cracked. Grief and sorrow spilled over. Burying her face in her hands, she sobbed. Her shoulders shook. Her body wrenched.

After a time, she became aware of Frederick's hand on her shoulder. Gradually, the trembling subsided, and her tears slowed.

"Please help her, Lord," the minister softly prayed. "Comfort her during this time of grief and sorrow. Give her grace to face the long, agonizing days ahead as she misses her daughter. Give her the peace You promised Your children."

Peace?

The word wandered through her mind as her tremors ceased. Was it possible to feel peace in a world so cruel and callous? Was it possible to find comfort amidst the pain and anguish of a people who faced such great loss and restless uncertainty?

She didn't know, but she suddenly longed to find out. She was tired of feeling empty and desolate. . .and alone.

Yes, even among the members of her clan and family, she felt lonely and desperately alone.

"He can give you the peace you're seeking," Frederick said, as though reading her mind. "All you have to do is believe in Him and ask Him to come into your life."

Raising her head, she looked into the minister's earnest eyes and saw a reflection of God's love born out of years of unwavering devotion to his faith. It humbled her and instilled in her the knowledge that God was real. She wanted more than anything to taste the sweetness of His mercy, experience the favor of His grace. But had she waited too long?

"I have rejected God for so long, Frederick. I have shaken my fist in His face out of anger over my people's removal. Why would He bother to listen to the prayer of someone like me?"

An understanding smile curved his lips. "Because His love is unconditional. What you have done in the past doesn't matter to Him. What you do with your life after you ask Him into your heart, the kind of witness you choose to be, will be what matters to Him. And you, Snowbird, being a respected principal of your clan, can lead many souls to Christ."

Although she was encouraged by the conviction in Frederick's voice, a remnant of doubt lingered. "I believed in Him once. It still seems forgiveness for someone like me is a lot to ask of Him."

"Snowbird, He sent His only Son to earth to die for the sins of the world. There is no sin you've committed that He isn't willing and ready to forgive. The price has already been paid. All He requires is that we confess and believe. He wants you to follow Him with a willing heart."

She gazed out over the blue-hued mountains. "I'm not sure I even know where to begin."

"How about at the beginning?"

In her peripheral vision, she saw him reach for something on his opposite side. Shifting her gaze, she found him holding a Bible in his grasp—Emily's Bible. Snowbird's chest ached.

"I've been reading some of Emily's favorite passages," he said. "She has them underlined. But I think nothing would please her more than for her mother to begin her walk with

Christ using the book she depended on so much."

Snowbird knew Emily would want that. She had heard her daughter whisper many prayers for her mother's soul in the past.

Snowbird stared at the small black Bible. Then, swallowing her choking grief, she reached out a trembling hand for the leather-bound book. She ran a calloused forefinger across the rough, worn cover.

"I think I'll head back to camp," the minister said. Giving her hand a pat, he rose and walked away.

Snowbird waited until she knew he was beyond hearing, then bowed her head and closed her eyes. "Lord, I have nothing to offer You but the time I have left here on earth. I know I've wasted many years in my anger and rejection of You, and I'm not worthy of Your forgiveness now, but I am asking for it. I promise from this day forward, I will do my best to serve You."

When she finished praying, she didn't experience a monumental change or a sudden exhilaration as she had expected. Instead, she felt a deep, calming sense of peace and the blessed assurance that her life had changed forever.

 છે

When Frederick had stood to leave, Marcus had ducked quietly behind a laurel thicket. Now he crouched silently, awestruck by what he'd just witnessed.

Since the first time he'd come to the Blue Haven in search of his daughter, he had felt compelled to pray for Snowbird. Before learning of Emily's death, he'd talked to Ethan about Snowbird and learned that the trials she had experienced during her lifetime had hardened her heart and shattered her belief in a fair and just God.

Marcus could see why. She and her people had suffered so much at the hands of his own people. Since Emily's death, he himself had questioned why God would take someone as young and pure. It seemed she had so much work to do with her children and her gift of medicinal healing.

Narrowing his eyes, Marcus chewed on his lower lip. Until now, he'd feared Emily's tragic death would only push Snowbird farther away from God. Perhaps the opposite was true. Perhaps losing Emily had brought Snowbird to her lowest point, a place where she had to choose to live for Christ or sink into never-ending despair.

If that should be the case, then perhaps Emily's death had not been in vain.

Marcus pressed a palm against the heaviness in his chest. His daughter's death still hurt. Even though he'd met Emily only once, she was still his flesh and blood—his daughter. And he'd loved her as such since the second he'd laid eyes on her. His grief over losing her couldn't have been greater if he'd known her all her life.

Then there were Jed and Julie. They had completely stolen his heart. Looking into their sad, dejected eyes almost brought him to his knees in grief.

He moved his hand from his chest to the nape of his neck and massaged tense muscles. He had to confess, he'd been throwing a few angry questions of his own toward God lately. Why had his father lied to him about Snowbird twenty-seven years ago? Why had she been forced to raise their children alone? Why had he been deprived of their childhood? Why had Snowbird been violated? Why had her people been robbed of their lands? Why did Emily have to die?

He recalled the answer Frederick had given Snowbird: evil.

The word floated across Marcus's mind like a dark cloud.

But You are mightier and stronger than evil, Lord. Why don't You release Snowbird and her people from the bondage evil has placed upon them? They are weak, tired, and so, so weary.

My grace is sufficient.

Marcus's shoulders slumped, not in defeat but in resignation. In the Bible, Paul was stricken with a thorn in his flesh, an unnamed infirmity. Three times he asked God to remove the thorn, but He didn't. Instead, He assured Paul His grace would be sufficient for Paul to endure the thorn, and that His strength would compensate for Paul's mortal weakness.

Marcus released a slow, silent sigh. If the trials of the removal were to remain, if Snowbird's destiny was to be lived out in this rugged wilderness, Marcus had some soul-searching of his own to do and some decisions to make.

Quietly he slipped out of the thicket and back to his shelter to pray.

seven

Snowbird slipped out of her shelter into the coolness of the early July night. The twins had fallen asleep with ease tonight, but restlessness still plagued Snowbird. Perhaps it was the full moon, shining so brightly the stars were barely visible against the canopy of soft blue sky.

Pressing her hands to the small of her back, she stretched her sore spine. Since her commitment to Christ a week ago, life in the camp hadn't changed, just as Frederick had predicted. The days were still long, hot, and grueling. Her people's situation was still demeaning.

But as Frederick had also predicted, her attitude had changed. Instead of prison walls keeping her from freedom and the life she once knew, she saw the great Appalachian Mountains surrounding her as a fortress protecting her and her people from evil. She no longer looked at the children in the camp and saw lives destined for pain and misery. Instead, she saw lives filled with hope of a brighter tomorrow—one where all people were free and treated as equals. Instead of wondering if her tired, weary body would hold up another day, she awakened each morning thanking God for the grace and strength He had promised her.

Her grief for her daughter was still raw, like an open wound that refused to heal. But Snowbird now had a deep-seated peace that she would somehow survive the heartache. And she was secure in the knowledge she now had a Friend who would never leave her nor forsake her.

Somewhere in the distance, the call of a lone whippoor-will broke the monotonous cadence of the cicadas and the soothing gurgle of a nearby stream. For once, the earth lay tranquil, wrapped in the essence of the moon's serene glow. Snowbird filled her lungs with a breath of sweet, soul-cleansing air. Yes, she was beginning to see the world through a different set of eyes.

Tugging her thin shawl tight around her shoulders, she meandered toward the outer edge of the camp, where she could walk among the shadows unnoticed by sleepless eyes.

The neigh of a corralled horse heightened Snowbird's senses. She stopped as a chill raced across her skin. She wasn't alone. Someone was watching her, and she knew exactly who.

"Marcus?"

He stepped from behind an aged white oak, his golden hair surrounding his head like an incandescent halo in the moonlight. With one hand, she grasped the front of her blouse, just beneath the high collar.

He sauntered forward, his features clearly visible in the intense moonlight. She tilted her head to look up at him.

A befuddled frown marred his forehead. "How did you know it was me?"

She blinked, then frowned. How had she known it was him? Was it the smell of his recently bathed skin? The scent of his newly laundered shirt? Had he stepped on a dry twig?

Her mouth dropped open as she searched for an appropriate response, but the words couldn't find their way past her tongue. For as she stood there, looking up at him in wide-eyed wonder, the hands of time reached out and peeled away the years, enlightening the memory of her and Marcus at Spring Place.

She had always known when he was near. She didn't have to see him, hear him, or even be expecting him. Instead, she possessed an innate ability to sense his presence long before he made an appearance. And twenty-seven years of separation had not changed anything—not even her love for him.

Her eyes widened in surprise. Surely she wasn't still in love with him.

But even as her practical sense of reasoning denied the realization, her heart told her the affection remained, awakening after almost three quiescent decades.

"You always knew, didn't you?" It was more of a statement than a question. "Back at Spring Place, you always knew exactly where I was long before you could see or hear me. Even after all these years, nothing has changed." Looking at her with something akin to awe, he reached out to touch her face.

Fighting her own willful instincts, she stepped back and turned away. "Don't be ridiculous, Marcus," she tossed back over her shoulder. "Everything has changed. We were hardly more than children then, caught up in a youthful fantasy of love. Now we're adults whose lives have gone in totally opposite directions."

She expected him to step up behind her and settle his hands on her shoulders or argue that something special still existed between them, as a young Marcus would have done. When no response came, in a tone of sternness and finality she added, "We each have responsibilities and obligations to our own people. Unfortunately, we fight for very different causes."

Another heartbeat passed, then, "You're right, of course."

So sudden was his change in direction, she spun back around to face him. To her surprise and chagrined disappointment, she found him standing, spine soldier straight, hands folded behind him. His stance, with his feet planted a shoulders' width apart, portrayed distinctly the commander he was born to be.

She opened her mouth to respond, then closed it, reminding herself he had agreed with her and she had no further reason for argument.

"We do have opposing responsibilities and obligations to our people," he added. "That's why I'll be leaving tomorrow. I've a pressing matter I need to attend to."

Leaving, she mused. Her mind carried her back to a small herb garden in Spring Place, and an unanticipated and sad acceptance settled over her. They would see each other from time to time because of the children. But when all was said and done, he would leave.

He would always be leaving.

"Then I will be returning to the Blue Haven," he said, dispelling her musings.

"I'm sure the children will be happy to see you any time you can get away from your duties long enough for a visit."

"Well, I would hope so, but the children aren't the only reason I'll be returning. And when I do return, it won't be for a visit."

She took a moment to consider his words, which made no sense. "I'm sorry, Marcus, I don't understand. Why would you be coming back, if not for a visit?"

"Because I'll be coming back to stay."

Intently he studied her, as though gauging her reaction.

She was still trying to figure out where he was headed with his reasoning when he added, "And to marry you."

For a long moment, she just stood there staring at him, allowing the meaning of his words to seep into her conscious. "Marry me?" she uttered in disbelief. Surely she had misunderstood.

He rocked back on his heels. "That's right."

Another small space in time stretched out, then hung between them like a fragile thread about to snap.

She took in his confident stance, his crooked grin, and decided he wasn't thinking clearly.

"Marcus, you're confused. I'm sure you'll see things differently when you return to your duties with the army." She turned and started back toward her shelter.

"Snowbird, wait!"

She whipped back around, and he caught her upper arms to keep from bumping into her.

"Keep your voice down!" she scolded in a whisper. "You'll wake the camp with your nonsense!"

She tried to wrench free of his hold, but he held on to her in an amazingly gentle but firm grasp. "Running away isn't going to change how we feel about each other."

Her struggling ceased. "We? I don't recall you asking me how I feel."

He shook his head in denial. "I didn't have to. You tell me with your eyes every time you look at me. A thousand butterflies take flight"—he raised a fisted hand to his chest—"right here."

His closeness challenged her ability to think clearly, so she focused on the fist pressed against his chest and reminded herself a relationship with Marcus would be doomed from the start. He was a soldier, she a Cherokee. Fate had crossed their paths, but it would never lead them in the same direction.

"Say you don't, Snowbird. Look into my eyes and say you don't love me."

I can do that, she thought. If it would put to rest his silly notion that they could have a life together, she could do just that.

Pulling a deep, fortifying breath, she lifted her gaze to his, and the words she intended to say stuck in her throat along with air trying to leave her lungs.

He smiled with satisfaction. "That's what I thought."

She expelled her pent-up breath and dropped her tense shoulders. He was a sly warrior. He knew how to choose his battles and how to fight to win. But surely he could be made to see the futility in this one.

"It doesn't matter what we feel for each other," she said. "You are a soldier. I am Cherokee." And that, she was certain, was enough to convince him he was pursuing something that could never be.

He urged her closer. "When I return to my post at Adela, I am going to draft a letter requesting my retirement."

She laid a palm on his chest where his heart beat strong and steady—calm. He was sure of his decision. . .for now.

But she knew the toll time could take on his sacrifices. Whatever she'd forgotten about Marcus Gunter, she hadn't forgotten this: He was born to be a soldier. That's why he'd left her so many years ago back in Spring Place. And why he would leave her again. Perhaps not physically, for he was a man of honor, and once he made a vow, he would never break it. But when he realized he'd given up his life's vocation for her, he would grow to resent their life together. Then his trapped spirit would die.

She wouldn't let that happened. Couldn't. As much as she loved him and longed so often lately for a life with him, her dreams would have to remain just that. Dreams. But she was going to have to make her argument a strong one if she was going to dissuade the stubborn man from pursuing her.

She took two quick steps back, breaking contact, and turned her back to him so she wouldn't have to look into his persuasive eyes when she spoke. "I've listened to you, Marcus. Now I want you to hear me out."

When he didn't respond, she continued. "In the last three months, my people and my family have been forced from their homes and land. My grandson almost died, and I've lost my daughter. And only a week ago, I committed my life to Christ and am trying to study His Word in order to make up for the many years I was lost in my rebellion.

"I do have feelings for you—I'll admit that. But to entertain the idea of marrying you would only place one more complication on my life, and I honestly don't think I could handle that right now."

Several long seconds passed in silence. Had he slipped away in the darkness?

Turning back around, she found he'd resumed his stance with his hands folded behind his back.

"One year," he said.

"One year?"

He gave a curt nod. "That should give me ample time to settle my affairs and you the time you need to adjust to your new life here and your new faith. As for losing Emily. . ." His voice thickened with grief. "You'll never stop missing her. But perhaps time will at least ease the pain a bit."

Snowbird shook her head in denial. "You've gone mad," she said, for that was all she could think to say.

One corner of his mouth tipped. "No, I haven't, Snowbird. I am simply pursuing our destiny."

eight

Winter that year was just as cold and brutal as the summer had been hot and dry. Four elders of the clan, including the clan chief, and one young child succumbed to its ruthless hand, which knocked the camp into near paralysis with its bitter winds, icy rain, and wet snow.

But with the new year came the promise that winter would eventually give way to the warm winds of spring and confirmation that life would prevail. In late January, Lillian gave birth to a dark-haired, fair-skinned baby girl. The infant reminded Snowbird so much of Emily, the doting grandmother sometimes wondered if God had sent the child to help fill the void left in her life after she lost her daughter.

Ethan and Lillian choose to name the babe Sara Emily, after her maternal grandmother and her late aunt. Snowbird took this as a sign of God's confirmation that He would provide the support the Walker family needed to get through their trials, both great and small.

In the meantime, Marcus continued to send supplies. But since his departure the previous summer, there had been no word or visit from him, even though Snowbird had sent a message to him after the birth of their grandchild. She could only assume he was still busy with the removal and could not procure a leave. Or that he had received the letter and chosen not to respond because he had nothing to say to Snowbird.

She tried not to dwell on his long silence. After all,

Frederick would have sent word if ill fate had fallen upon the colonel. Most likely, when he'd returned to his post and regained command of his regiment, he'd realized he was where he wanted to be, doing what he loved to do. Be a soldier.

She'd never expected him to follow through on his impulsive proposal anyway. Marcus Gunter live in the wilderness with a horde of rebellious Indians? The mere thought of that ever happening brought a sad smile to Snowbird's lips.

❧

June 1839

"Riders coming in!" the Cherokee watchman called.

Snowbird stumbled, almost dropping the basket of heavy, wet clothes she was carrying back from the lake. One of the riders, she knew, was Marcus. For two days now, an overwhelming sense of restlessness had plagued her, forewarning her that his arrival was near.

She set the basket down near the clothesline and straightened, using her hand to shield her eyes from the morning sun. Jed and Julie, who had become extremely cautious and protective since their mother's death, ran from where they were playing in the shade and tucked themselves in close on each side of Snowbird.

Hanging back with the twins, Snowbird watched as Billy, Lillian, and Ethan, who proudly cradled little Sara in one arm, gathered with the crowd to welcome the riders. When Billy turned and motioned her forward, she shook her head, placing a protective hand on a shoulder of each grandchild. The twins pressed in closer. Snowbird felt the tug of Jed's hand as he bunched her skirt in a small, strong fist.

Breathing heightened, she waited for the riders. What news would Marcus bring to her? Had he left the army and come back as determined to marry her as he had been almost a year ago? Or had he decided his love for his country and the military reached deeper than the love he felt for her?

In a few long seconds, she had her answer, for the first rider was Marcus, and he was dressed in full campaign uniform.

❧

Marcus was exhausted. He and Frederick had ridden from sunup to sundown for nine weeks, stopping only to rest their horses, eat, and sleep. He was desperate for a refreshing, cleansing bath and a soft pillow on which to rest his head. But before he could rest, he had an urgent message to deliver to Snowbird.

His eyes, though windburned and travel-weary, were drawn to a place beyond the gathering crowd.

Snowbird stood back away from the others, a protective arm around her seven-year-old grandchildren. Her green dress was faded and tattered. Her shoulders appeared thinner than the last time he'd seen her. Yet she stood straight and proud. A tower of strength among a broken people.

"Papa?"

Marcus looked down to find his adopted daughter, Lillian, standing beside his horse. Next to her stood her husband, Ethan, holding their daughter. Marcus quickly calculated the information he'd received in Snowbird's letter. The child would be five months old now. A thick crop of dark hair framed her round cherubic face. Her onyx eyes targeted him with sparkling curiosity. Her chin glistened with dribble while she gummed a chubby fist.

Heart swelling with pride, Marcus smiled, and some of his

trail-weariness left him. "So this is my little princess," he said as he dismounted.

"Yes, Colonel." Ethan stepped forward, placing the child in Marcus's arms. "Meet Sara Emily."

"Sara Emily," Marcus repeated. "You've named her well."

While Marcus would have liked to take the present time to get to know his granddaughter, the reason for his visit to the Indian camp remained foremost in his mind. "She is beautiful," he said, passing the happy, giggling babe back to her father. "A perfect angel. And later, I will enjoy treating her as such." He brushed her pink cheek with a forefinger. "But first"—he glanced up at Ethan—"I must talk to your mother."

His gaze drifted back to Snowbird, still standing in the distance with her arms anchored around her grandchildren's shoulders. A tumbleweed of conflicting emotions bounced around his stomach. The news he had to deliver would thrill her. Then it would break her heart all over again.

❧

Snowbird watched Marcus approach, the gilded hilt of his saber throwing out sharp slashes of reflected sunlight with each deliberate step he took. She straightened her spine a little more, lifted her chin a bit higher. She wasn't surprised he'd decided to remain a soldier. In fact, she'd expected it.

But she hadn't expected his change of heart to hurt her so.

Tensing her jaw and drawing in a deep breath of fortitude, she was determined not to let him see her enormous disappointment.

He stopped in front of her and plucked his tall hat from his head. First, he greeted his grandchildren, Jed and Julie; then he met Snowbird's gaze. Dark circles haunted his eyes. Lines of weariness creased the corners of his mouth. And he'd lost weight. She didn't want to put off the inevitable but didn't have the heart to press him to proceed with their impending conversation.

"You look tired, Marcus," she said. "Why don't you rest for a while? Then we can talk."

"My news can't wait." He glanced down at the twins. "Do you mind staying with your Uncle Ethan and Aunt Lillian while I talk with your grandmother?"

The children looked up at Snowbird through huge, dark eyes filled with questions. She nodded her approval. Reluctantly, they released her skirt, clasped hands, and traipsed off toward Ethan and Lillian.

"Let's go sit in the shade, shall we?" Marcus motioned toward the shadowed, spotty grass beneath a nearby oak.

She really didn't want to sit down. She wanted to stand so she could make a hasty retreat should her emotions overcome her. "That isn't necessary, Marcus. I understand that you've changed your mind, and I'm all right with you decision."

"I haven't changed my mind, Snowbird. And that isn't why I'm here. I have some news." He hesitated, as though weighing carefully his next words. "It's about Emily."

Snowbird's heart skipped a beat. "Emily?"

"Yes." He captured her upper arm, steadying her. "Please." Gently, he urged her toward the shade.

On wobbly legs, she walked to the patchy grass and gratefully accepted his assistance as she sat down. She couldn't fathom what Marcus had to tell her about Emily. Had someone robbed her grave? Disturbed her body? Snowbird grasped Marcus's forearm as he settled next to her. "What about Emily?"

He turned so he faced her, clasping her hands in his. "She's alive."

Snowbird's world slammed to an abrupt halt. Even the wind ceased moving. For at least five long seconds, all she heard was her heartbeat pounding in her ears.

"Alive?" she finally managed to utter.

He nodded.

"You've seen her?"

Again he nodded, and beyond the weariness haunting his eyes, she found confirmation.

Her pent-up breath left her in an exhilarating rush. She threw her arms around his neck. He, in response, embraced her in a crushing hug. Her laughter filled the air with joy.

"Oh, Marcus. Marcus, that's wonderful."

As quickly as she had grabbed him, she pushed back, settling her hands on his chest. He rested his palms on her waist.

"Is she all right?" Snowbird wanted to know. "Has anyone. . . harmed her?"

The corners of his tired eyes and mouth crinkled. "She's fine and well into the Arkansas Territory by now."

"So she was removed with the rest of our captured people?"

"Yes, she was. But when I found her, the detachment she was traveling with had almost reached the end of the trail, and she was actually nursing a young army lieutenant back to health."

The wheels of planning began spinning in Snowbird's head. She gathered the front of his shirt in her fists. "How are we going to get her home? How soon can you offer her safe passage?"

The light of celebration in Marcus's eyes faded. He reached up and cupped her fists in his hands.

She read his solemn actions. Sweat dampened her palms and

the skin above her lips. Her joy drizzled back down to hope.

"She is home," Marcus said.

"What do you mean, 'She is home'? She belongs here with her family."

"No, my love. She belongs there, in the Arkansas Territory, with her new husband."

Snowbird's hold on Marcus's shirt slackened. Her hands slipped from his grasp and collapsed on her lap in a limp heap. "Husband?"

❧

Marcus looked into the eyes of the woman he loved. How would she receive what he had to say next—as a blessing or betrayal? "Yes. She's married to the young soldier she was nursing back to health when I found her. He wrote to me a few months ago and told me she was alive and needed to be returned to her family. When I caught up with them on the trail, it didn't take long to figure out how deeply in love they were."

He hesitated several dreaded heartbeats, giving her time to absorb his words while he summoned the courage to say the next. "I encouraged her to stay and not repeat the mistake I made twenty-eight years ago."

"And she agreed, even though her children are here?"

He swallowed hard. "I promised I'd bring the children to her. She and her new husband feel they have a work to do in the West. Jon—that's his name—is going to leave the army and become a minister, and they are going to build a church for her people."

Suspended seconds passed. Then to Marcus's surprise, she gave a small nod of acceptance. "If that's where God has led her, then that's where she should be."

❧

"Grandma, why can't you go with us?" came Julie's small voice.

From across the supper table, Marcus watched as Snowbird placed a piece of corn bread on her granddaughter's plate. The attentive grandmother sat with a twin flanking each side.

"Because your uncle Billy needs me to stay here and take care of him," Snowbird told the child.

The comment drew everyone's attention to Snowbird's seventeen-year-old son sitting on Julie's other side. He pretended to hit his tin mug with his hand, spilling a few drops of milk but catching it just before it completely toppled over.

Picking up on Billy's attempt to cheer up the inquisitive child, Snowbird shook her head, stood, pulled a dishcloth from the waistband of her skirt, and wiped up the liquid.

"She's right, little one," Billy said. "She has to stay here and clean up my spills."

The playful caper brought a round of laughter from the group of Cherokee assembled around the Walker family table, save one. While Snowbird's lips lifted in a quiet smile, her eyes bespoke the sadness she felt from Jed and Julie's impending departure.

Still, she put on a cheery facade for her grandchildren's sake. "You know your uncle Billy, Julie. I'll probably still be patching up his cuts and scrapes when he's thirty."

Marcus continued to observe in wonder. While Billy's ever-buoyant personality could lift the dreariest of moods, he was among the hardest workers in the camp. Marcus had also noticed the lad possessed the invaluable qualities of a leader. No doubt, he would succeed in whatever he endeavored to do with his life.

The colonel turned his attention back to Snowbird, who

was now back in her seat and filling Jed's plate. As she had for the past three days since he'd been there, she made all the right comments, told jokes when appropriate, even laughed a time or two.

But those sad, dark eyes of hers opened the windows to her soul and told Marcus she was already bleeding loneliness inside for her grandchildren.

Marcus's thoughts skipped forward. Tomorrow was the day she would watch them ride away with him, not knowing when or if she would ever see them again in this life.

How would she hold up after he was gone? Marcus had to try and find out.

With the backs of his knees, he slid his chair away from the table and stood. "Snowbird, would you honor me with your presence for a walk this evening?"

Obviously taken aback by his request, she blinked up at him. "We. . .we. . .ah. . .shouldn't we finish supper first?"

"I don't think either of us is interested in eating tonight."

She glanced down, first at one plate of uneaten food, then the other, then back up at him. "What about cleaning up?"

"Ethan and Billy can take care of that while Lillian watches the children."

Billy, who had been watching the exchange with interest, gave Marcus a grin, a salute, and a hearty, "Yes, sir."

Tossing his homemade napkin next to his plate, Marcus sauntered around the oak table and held out his arm.

With what appeared to be a sliver of trepidation, she rose and slipped her small, work-roughened hand into the crook of his arm.

❧

A thin thread of impatience wove through Snowbird. She

didn't want to miss a single minute of the precious few hours she had left with her grandchildren. But she owed Marcus a few minutes of her time. She'd been so caught up in preparing Jed and Julie for their journey west that she hadn't even taken time to thank Marcus for bringing her the wonderful news about Emily.

He led her through the layer of forest toward the lake. As they stepped into the clearing on the lakeshore, a doe and her spotted young fled. A fish broke the water's surface, sending a shimmering ring of ripples across the otherwise still water.

He guided her to the bathing rock and stopped. She stood beside him, looking across the lake where the setting sun burned the cloudless sky in a blaze of orange-red. While she waited long seconds for him to speak, she became acutely aware of his presence. The way the fine hair of his forearm below his rolled-up sleeve felt beneath her hand. How his side rose and fell against her elbow with each breath he took. The smell of his sun-kissed skin. A sudden rush of heat reached her cheeks.

Reminding herself she had neither the time nor convenience to entertain thoughts of loving him, she pulled her arm away from his and took two steps forward. "Tomorrow will be clear. The wind is coming down from the northeast. It should be a pleasant day to start your journey."

She waited for his response, and when he gave none, she turned and almost crumbled beneath the weight of sadness in his eyes. "Marcus, what's wrong?"

"Snowbird, I am so sorry I'm taking Jed and Julie away from you."

Forcing a smile, she stepped back up to him. "You're not taking them away from me. Besides, they're not mine to hold on to. They belong with their mother."

He studied her so intently, she feared he could see the pain lodged in her throat.

Slowly, he shook his head. "This can't be easy for you."

Nothing ever is, she thought, then silently scolded herself for her self-pity. She had survived thus far. With God's help, she would survive this latest loss, as well.

Reaching up, she framed his face with her hands. A day's growth of beard pricked her palms. She looked deeply into his eyes, wanting to ease his worried mind. "It's true I will miss the children. But knowing their mother is alive and that they will soon be reunited with her will ease my loneliness in the days to come."

She paused, giving him time to absorb her words. "Thank you, Marcus Gunter, for bringing the news that our daughter is alive. Thank you for taking her children to her. Knowing they will be traveling with you will be a great comfort to me. I know you'll protect them with your life."

She studied his tender expression, not completely confident she'd convinced him she'd be all right when he left.

The feel of one of his hands on her waist and the other brushing a stray tendril of hair away from her face tilted her world.

All at once, his eyes filled with tears. "I love you so much," he rasped. He swallowed, as though trying to clear something stuck in his throat. "I can hardly bear the thought of leaving you tomorrow. But I promise this time will be the last."

She wanted to believe him. Wanted to with all her heart. But there was a definite truth staring her in the face. She slid her hands down to his chest. Her gaze followed and fixed on the shiny buttons of his uniform vest. "Marcus, please don't make a promise you can't keep."

With a thumb under her chin, he tipped her head up, forcing her to look at him. "The other day, when I told you I hadn't changed my mind, I meant it. My release has been requested and approved. I asked that it be delayed until the end of the year. It will be safer for Jed and Julie to travel with an army officer than a civilian. Now there's only one question to be answered." With the agility of a young buck, he dropped to one knee. "The night I told you I intended to marry you, you told me I hadn't bothered to ask you how you feel. Well, now I'm asking. Snowbird Walker, will you marry me?"

She couldn't breathe. Couldn't think. Couldn't speak.

Her emotions told her she wanted to marry him more than she wanted to draw her next breath. But she had lost so many things she'd loved, beginning with her loss of him twenty-eight years ago. She didn't know if she could open her heart up to that kind of vulnerability again. She didn't know if she wanted to.

"Marcus," she finally managed to say, "I—I don't know what to say."

"Just say you'll be here, waiting for me when I return."

She gave a small nod. She knew she would be waiting whether he returned or not. She would wait for him forever.

He rose and gathered her in an embrace that bespoke a promise—a promise that had been waiting to be fulfilled for twenty-eight years.

nine

Five months later

Two riders and their mounts moved like glistening shadows through the cold, damp fog blanketing the Appalachian Mountains. Each breath of horse and man was an icy vapor that curled in the frost before being sucked up by the approaching dawn.

With every other sway of the lead animal, a blinding glint off the gilded hilt of the saber on the first rider's hip pierced the darkness, as the half-moon's beam slipped through the craggy naked branches of the towering hardwoods and shivering pines.

The silence was deafening except for the creak in the second rider's leather saddle and the soft padding whisper of horses' hooves on dew-drenched leaves.

Something moved among the shadows. The first rider raised his hand as though in greeting. A bright, hot flash seared the air. The first rider's limp body slid from his horse's back to the cold, hard ground.

❧

Snowbird's eyes snapped open. Her head lay on a sweat-drenched blanket pillow. Her damp, clammy body shook. Like that of a frightened bird, her racing heart fluttered inside her chest. Each quickened breath left her lips in a frosty vapor.

Three times she'd had this dream—Marcus returning to the valley to be with her. But this one had been different. Not like the first two, which had been full of hope, promises fulfilled, and sunlight. This one had been dark and full of imminent danger.

She slung back heavy layers of blankets and scrambled into her moccasins. Grabbing her shawl from the corner basket, she slipped outside her shelter and ran through the cold, wet night to Ethan's tent.

He emerged through his shelter's flap door as she approached. With his keen sense of hearing and innate ability to sense peril, his sleep had obviously been disturbed.

Snowbird's elder son steadied his mother by capturing her upper arms. "What's wrong?"

"I had a dream."

He narrowed his eyes. "The colonel?"

She nodded.

"Tell me."

She told him about all three dreams and how the last differed from the first two. Grasping the front of her son's buckskin shirt, she added, "I fear he may be in trouble, Ethan. I must find a way to get to him."

He gave a single nod of acknowledgment. "I'll leave at first light."

Another fear squeezed in next to the one she felt for Marcus's welfare—that of losing her son. "No! You have a wife and daughter who need you. I'll go alone."

"Don't be ridiculous, Mother. Besides, Marcus is also my wife's father and my daughter's grandfather. Who better to go than me?"

"How about me?"

Both heads turned as Billy stepped from the shadows. Fingers tucked into his trouser pockets, he shuffled up to his mother and brother.

"You'll do no such thing!" Snowbird scolded.

He shrugged a shoulder. "Why not? Ethan's family needs him. The clan needs you. My duties here aren't so. . .specific."

Because Billy was conceived as the result of a brutal attack on Snowbird, he felt he didn't quite fit in or belong anywhere. If he only knew how many lives he'd touched with his ready grin and encouraging personality.

While Ethan was a solid tower of strength, Billy was an overflowing river of joy to all who knew him. And Snowbird didn't love either of her sons above the other.

She broke free of Ethan and laid a hand on Billy's smooth cheek. "Billy, you are the one who holds us all together and keeps us from losing our sanity."

He grinned a dimpled grin. "Which is exactly why I need to find Marcus and bring him back to you. So you will not go crazy on us."

Snowbird's eyes burned. "Billy, if something were to happen to you, I couldn't bear it." She shook her head. "I won't let you go."

Billy looked to his older brother. "Help me pack. I leave at first light."

Turning on his heel, he headed toward the corral.

A chill passed through Snowbird. "I'll go with you." She ran after him.

Ethan stopped her by capturing her arm. "Let him go, Mother. He needs to do this."

Snowbird stopped short of arguing and studied her elder son's shadowed features. There, she read his silent message.

Billy needed to prove he was a man worthy of taking care of his family. It was his time. Reluctantly, Snowbird nodded.

Ethan left to follow his brother. When Ethan was beyond eyesight, Snowbird went back to her shelter, fell down on her knees, and began to pray.

ॐ

"Rider coming in!"

Snowbird's cold, stiff hand stilled on the cow's warm udder. The steady *shush-shush-shush* sound of milk hitting foamy liquid in her pail stopped.

Billy had been gone two weeks—fourteen short days. Not long when a scout was searching the Appalachians for someone. But for a mother waiting for a son to return safely from hostile territory and a woman waiting news of the man she loved, that last fourteen days had seemed almost an eternity.

She challenged herself not to get too excited. After all, the rider could be one of the friendly white men who occasionally delivered news to and from the outside. She wiped her hands on her apron, set aside her handmade stool, and stood, stretching the soreness out of her back. Then, watching the entrance to the dale, she picked up her milk pail and carried it to the table on the east side of the camp, where most of the food was prepared. As she was setting down the pail, the rider appeared.

Billy!

Eyes stinging with tears of relief, Snowbird lifted her skirts and ran to meet him. The dead, frosty grass crackled beneath her single-seam moccasins.

As he slipped off his painted stallion, she threw her arms around his neck. He caught her up in a hug that left her feet dangling a foot off the ground.

"Thank God, you are home," she whispered a prayer.

When he set her back on her feet, she drew back, framing his cool, smooth face with her hands. She studied his weary features for reassurance he'd returned unharmed. Satisfied he was all right, she allowed her gaze to settle on his and found deep sadness.

Her heart kicked against her chest. "Marcus?" Her soft voice reached for a sliver of hope.

Billy looked over his mother's head and motioned to Ethan and Lillian, who had been waiting patiently to speak to Billy. Lillian passed a sleeping Sara to a young maiden's waiting arms; then she, Ethan, and Snowbird followed Billy to the north end of the camp, away from the gathered crowd.

Snowbird, Ethan, and Lillian stood hand in hand, waiting for Billy to speak.

"He's alive," the young scout finally said.

"Oh, thank You, God!" Lillian cried, then clamped her free hand over her mouth.

Ethan released his wife's hand and slipped a supportive arm around her.

But Snowbird stood upright, afraid to breathe, for she knew from the serious expression on her younger son's face there was more.

Billy gave Lillian a few seconds to regain control of her emotions, then continued. "He and Frederick are with an older couple in the foothills." He fixed his gaze on his mother. "You were right. He has been wounded. He was shot by a Cherokee man who had escaped his detachment and was making his way back east to try and find his family. The Indian apparently thought Marcus and Frederick were soldiers scouting for runaways.

"Before Frederick could be shot, he was able to convince the Indian they meant him no harm. So the Indian gave them directions to the cabin. Apparently, this couple has been supplying some of the refugees with food."

Snowbird forced herself to swallow so she could speak. "Is Marcus going to be all right?"

"Physically, yes. . ." He allowed a small, bracing space of time to pass. "The wound was to his right arm. The village doctor couldn't save it."

Lillian broke down again, but Snowbird, sensing there was still more to Billy's news, kept her spine rigid. "I must go to him."

For a few seconds, Billy didn't respond, just stood stone-cold still and silent. Then, in a voice saturated with compassion, he said, "I'm afraid it's too late, Mother."

Frowning, she shook her head in both confusion and denial. "Too late? You said he was alive."

"He is." Billy slipped his hand inside his coat and withdrew a folded parchment. "He asked me to give this to you."

Snowbird stared at the parchment for a long time before reaching for it. The yellowed paper crackled in her cold hand as she grasped it between her thumb and the tips of her fingers. Then, stepping away from her family, she opened the letter she knew held a dark message.

The writing looked elementary, as if an unsteady hand had written it. Still, she recognized the curl on the bottom of the *S* in *Snowbird* and the curve at the end of the *d* as Marcus's handwriting. Since he'd lost his right arm, he'd obviously had to pen the letter with his left hand.

A picture of Marcus sitting at a stranger's table by dim

candlelight, struggling to write with his weaker hand, came to Snowbird's mind, and overwhelming sadness crushed her chest. Struggling to breathe, she grasped the collar of her blouse and fought to keep control of her tattered emotions. She and Marcus had survived tragedy and separation before, and they'd survive this one.

Drawing in a deep breath of fortitude, she began to read.

My dearest Snowbird,

Regrettably, I cannot marry you. As we both know, your calling is there in the village to your people. I have now realized mine is to my plantation, my home in Virginia, and to the people I employ there.

Tell Lillian I love her and look forward to seeing her and young Sara again someday.

You have my prayers and best wishes in your quest for freedom.

My kindest regards,
Marcus

Disbelief attacked Snowbird's mind. She turned and found Billy standing waiting nearby, watching her. She held up the letter. "Are you sure he wrote this?"

Billy nodded. "I was witness to it."

Inside the stunned silence, Snowbird's world began to crumble. An old, deep wound cracked open and started to bleed. So that was it. No life with Marcus. No wedding. A final separation.

The young hopes and dreams she'd finally ventured to reach for vanished like a vapor swept away by the wind. Her legs turned to water and a piece of her heart to stone. She had to get away from everyone. Be alone. Think. Weep. Grieve.

Breathe, she reminded herself. *Breathe, breathe, breathe!*

She released the grasp she held on her blouse and wiped her palm on her apron. "Well," she said, "I guess I'll get back to work before the milk spoils."

She forced her legs to carry her to her daughter-in-law and son, who were still consoling each other. "I am so sorry about your father's arm," Snowbird said. "I'm sure he'll get the best care in Virginia. We must remember that he's still alive. He still has his life."

Lillian nodded and swiped a hand across her wet face. "I know." She sniffed. "I wish I could be there for him."

Snowbird gave her daughter-in-law's arm what she hoped was an encouraging squeeze. "I know. As soon as Sara is a little older and things settle down outside the valley, I'm sure you can be."

She offered Lillian an embrace, then somehow, on legs that seemed to no longer exist, she walked away.

ten

Three months later, on a brisk afternoon marked by hints of spring, Frederick and another trusted white man arrived at the camp bearing two letters. One, Frederick passed to Lillian, the other to Snowbird. The minister's wife, Emma, penned the envelopes.

As Snowbird stood among her people, staring at the parchment envelope trapped between her thumb and forefinger, trepidation filled her mind. *Dear God,* she silently prayed, *please don't let it be bad news. Please let Marcus be all right.*

Over the past three months, she'd come to accept the painful reality that she and Marcus would never have a life together as husband and wife. She'd also accepted that separation, no matter how vast and long, would never change her love for him. That was an agonizing reality, a sacrificial cross, she must bear.

"Are you all right, Mother?"

She blinked up at Billy, who seemed to always be nearby in her times of stress. Always looking out for her.

Slipping the envelope into her apron pocket, she smiled at her son and the minister standing beside him. "Of course. I'm sure Miss Emma is just writing to give us an update on Marcus." She looked to Frederick for confirmation, but his expression gave her nothing. Apparently he was going to let the letter explain the reason for his unannounced visit.

"I'm sure she's done just that," Billy injected, then motioned his head toward Frederick's riding companion. "This is Ben

107

Nelms. He works at Marcus's plantation. I'm going to find him and Fred something to eat and take care of their horses. Then I'll get them settled in our guest quarters so they can rest awhile." Grinning, he winked at his reference to their guest quarters, a humble canvas shelter. "Why don't you take a walk, rest your mind a bit?"

"Thank you, Billy," she said. He'd just relieved her of her hostess duties. "I think I will."

Glancing over her shoulder from time to time, Snowbird slipped down to the lake. She didn't want anyone to follow. She'd share the contents of the letter with her family later. The first reading, however, she wanted to do alone.

Eager to learn Emma's message to her, Snowbird sat down on the bathing rock where the afternoon sun had warmed the stone and opened the envelope. Legs crisscrossed, lower lip trapped between her teeth, she began to read.

> *Dear Snowbird,*
> *I hope this letter finds you and your people well. Frederick and I are both doing well and have temporarily moved to Williamsburg in an attempt to see Marcus through his recovery, which, I'm afraid, isn't going so well.*

Snowbird stopped reading long enough to close her eyes and take a deep, bracing breath. This was not what she'd wanted to hear.

Opening her eyes, she continued to read.

> *That is the reason I am writing this letter to you, my dear friend. I hope you can forgive me for the selfish request I am about to ask of you.*

A sense of trepidation stole over Snowbird. What could Emma want her to do?

For six weeks now, I have tried to coax my brother out of the deep state of depression he has fallen into. But with each passing day, it becomes more apparent to me that I am not what he needs.

While his wound continues to heal nicely, his heart, I fear, is an entirely different matter. The loss of his arm has made him a very bitter, very angry man—not at all the confident, considerate brother I've known for so many years. He often refuses to eat and most days refuses to leave his room. Clearly, he feels useless and worthless, trapped in some torturous mental prison that neither Frederick nor I can penetrate.

What I find most interesting, however, are the things he says when he manages to catch a few hours' fitful slumber. He speaks to you.

Snowbird blinked twice. Marcus spoke to her? In his sleep? Head creased in concentration, she read on.

He says things like "I'm sorry I let you down. I'm sorry I can't take care of you. I'm no longer a whole man. I'll always love you."

A shudder passed through Snowbird's body. "And I'll always love you, Marcus," she whispered. "Always."

Snowbird, sometimes he goes on with this gibberish half the night. And sometimes, when he thinks no one is listening, he buries his head in his pillow and cries and prays the most heartbreaking prayers. He even questions why God didn't take his life.

Oh, Snowbird, Frederick told me of your and Marcus's past love for each other and how Marcus couldn't wait to get back to your village and claim your hand. However, the accident apparently changed all of that in his eyes. After he awakened from his surgery and realized he'd lost his arm, it was then he decided to return here, to his plantation. He told Frederick he'd not become a burden to anyone, especially to a woman who had already faced enough tragedy to fill ten lifetimes.

I am at my wit's end, Snowbird, and don't know what else to do. I fear my brother needs you, and I know your people need you. So please search your heart and do what you feel led to do.

Please know, as always, our thoughts and prayers are with you. I will accept whatever you decide as God's will.

With kindest regards,
Emma

Snowbird stared at the letter for a long time, even after she'd finished reading. Should she believe what Emma had written?

Ever since she'd received the letter from Marcus telling her he'd changed his mind about marrying her, she'd put aside all hopes of a future with him. The sting of his rejection, especially at a time when she thought he needed her most, had burned her quick and deep. She'd decided she'd never open herself to that kind of pain again. She couldn't bear it.

And now this?

She lifted her gaze to the lake, now split by sunlight and mountain shadows. Suppose she did go to Virginia? Could she somehow reach Marcus, draw him out of the anger and bitterness brought upon him by his loss of limb and feelings of inadequacy?

Reaching up with one hand, she grasped the front of her faded blue blouse, just below the high collar. She'd been that angry and bitter, and no one had been able to reach her except God. And that had taken years.

She dragged in a heavy breath, then released it on a weary sigh. Her family had been understanding and patient, though. Through all her years of rejection of and rebellion against Christ, they'd never given up on her.

Neither had God.

Maybe that's what Marcus needed: a lot of patience and a lot of prayer. Time.

But did he really need her presence, too? After all, she could pray for him in her valley just as well as she could at his home in Virginia. Distance wouldn't make a difference where prayer was concerned.

Her eyes slid closed. "Dear God, what should I do?"

"I think you should go."

Startled, her eyes snapped open as she twisted around. "Billy! You startled me. How long have you been standing there?"

He shrugged a shoulder. "Maybe a minute." He strolled over and eased down beside her, stretching out a long leg, folding the other, and resting his forearm on his knee.

Puzzled, Snowbird studied her son, who gazed out over the water. "Where, exactly, do you think I should go?"

"To Virginia to take care of Marcus."

"And just how did you find out what was in my letter?"

"Lillian shared the contents of hers with Ethan and me."

"I see." Snowbird swept a strand of wind-tossed hair behind her ear. "What I don't see is how I can abandon our people right now."

Serious for once, Billy met his mother's gaze. "You have devoted your life to your children and our people. Now the man you've loved for more than half your life needs you, and whether you want to admit it or not, you need him."

"What about our people? Who—"

"Ethan. He's perfectly capable of taking over the leadership of the clan. And he's more than ready."

Snowbird knew Billy was right. Ethan had proved himself capable of leading their people many times over the past year—times when Snowbird had been paralyzed by grief. When her daughter had been captured and thought to be dead. When her grandson had been deathly sick. When the twins left to go west. And most recently, when she'd received news that Marcus was wounded along with the letter telling her that he no longer wanted to marry her.

During these times, Ethan had stepped in and taken over the responsibilities of the clan's leader without hesitation. No doubt he could do the same in her absence.

Still, Snowbird had reservations. "What about you, Ethan, Lillian, and little Sara? How could I leave you here?"

"Other than missing you, I'm sure Ethan, Lillian, and little Sara will be fine. As for me, I'm going with you."

She opened her mouth to protest.

"Don't argue with me, Mother. Just accept that, right now, with you is where I'm supposed to be."

How could she argue with him when he put his reasoning that way?

Both stared out over the lake while Snowbird thought of

what a trip to Virginia would mean. Possibly six weeks on the road, but spring was upon them. They would have to travel under some sort of guise, but it could be managed. Billy would be with her, so she wouldn't be a lone female traveling with unrelated men. And Ethan would lead the clan.

Having reasoned around all the obstacles, she couldn't find a convincing excuse not to go.

She looked up to the heavens, silently asking God for confirmation, and found it in the deep peace that touched her soul. Still, as she decided to step onto this new path God had placed before her, her young faith wavered.

"What if I fail, Billy?" She voiced her most vulnerable thoughts. "What if I go, and neither God nor I nor all the prayers in the world can get through to Marcus? What happens then?"

"Then you will know you tried."

eleven

"It won't be very long now. Just around the next bend."

Snowbird turned her attention from the gently rolling green land beyond the carriage window to Frederick, who sat on the seat across from her. Since she had nothing of value to add to his comment, she offered him a quiet smile and turned her attention back to the unfamiliar world beyond the coach's window.

Billy, who preferred wide-open spaces to the confines of the carriage shell, had ridden up top during most of their journey, sharing driving duties with their traveling companion, Mr. Nelms.

The journey had been long and tiring but uneventful. They had traveled by horse over the roughest Appalachian terrain, then switched over to the carriage as they neared civilization. Frederick had worn his collar, and Snowbird had suffered through wearing her hair up in a tight bun, topping it off with a handmade bonnet. She and Billy had also traded their handmade moccasins for the store-bought shoes they had worn prior to their Blue Haven days.

To the people they met along the way, the wary foursome looked like members of a family traveling to some unknown destination. Not even the soldiers they had occasionally encountered stopped them to question their intentions.

As the carriage rounded the bend, Snowbird tipped her head forward to take in the unfolding view. A bright early-afternoon sun clothed the land in a radiant luster.

The two-story plantation house sat upon the gently rolling hill like a benevolent queen watching over her kingdom. The blanket of green she rested on served as her velvet-covered throne; the red brick adorning her, her ruby-colored robe of satin; the two-step front porch with its high white columns her footstool. The four chimneys topping the roof could have been the jewels of her regal crown.

With the four paneled windows and a massive wooden door on the first floor, and five gabled windows lining the second floor, she looked out over the southern end of her kingdom with quiet grace and dignity.

Elegant, Snowbird mused, *yet simple in adornment with its straight lines on the house and simple curves in the landscape.*

Snowbird was impressed, but she'd seen grander homes occupied by some of her very own people. Those fine homes were now occupied by the white men or lay in ruins, burned to the ground.

She felt the familiar blades of hate and anger slice through her. Closing her eyes, she said a silent prayer, putting to rest those often invasive demons of spiritual warfare.

As the horses pulling the carriage turned between the two brick columns marking the entrance to the property, Snowbird opened her eyes and studied the vast hills of grandeur. Tulip poplars, massive oaks, hickory, and magnolia trees adorned the soft roll of green land surrounding the house. Lower-growing boxwoods were arranged neatly around the front courtyard, and the flower and rose garden on the east side of the house would make any majesty proud.

I have no right to be here, she told herself. *This property belonged to Marcus and his dead wife.* Snowbird felt uneasy, like an intruder invading a strange land.

Yet as the carriage drew to a stop in the brick lane that circled in front of the house, Snowbird felt she'd finally reached her destination after a three-decade-long journey. An odd chill, then a calming warmth passed through her.

Billy opened the carriage door and extended his right hand to his mother. As she stepped out of the coach, she found Emma waiting for them on the wide front porch. Lifting the front of her blue cotton skirt a few inches, the minister's wife glided down the front steps like a feather floating downstream, in spite of her stout frame.

After greeting her husband and Billy with an enthusiastic hug, she then turned to Snowbird and gathered her up in a suffocating embrace. When Emma drew back, tears streamed down her rounded cheeks. "I will never be able to repay you for coming," she said as she clasped Snowbird's hands.

"No repayment of any kind is expected. I just hope I can be of help in some way."

"Trust me, dear, if anyone can reach down into this black hole my brother has fallen into and pull him out, you can."

"Only with God's help," Snowbird reminded, glancing up at the second-story windows and wondering if one belonged to Marcus. . .if he perhaps stood just beyond a closed curtain, looking down at them. But she didn't sense his presence as she had in the past whenever he was nearby. *Why?* she wondered. Was it because his spirit had died, or because he truly no longer loved her?

Snowbird pushed the last thought to the back of her mind. The first time Marcus had proposed to her in the mountain village, he'd challenged her to look him in the eye and deny her love for him. She couldn't do it. And she would believe he no longer loved her only when he could do the same.

She looked back at Emma with a melancholy smile. "Marcus needs our prayers more than anything."

"Those prayers, my dear, are exactly why I believe you are here. Come." Dropping one hand, Emma led Snowbird up the wide brick steps. "Let's get you freshened up and fed; then we'll go take on the beast."

෪

Two years.

That's how long it had been since Snowbird had taken a hot bath or bathed in anything more than a cold lake or stream. Now, as two months of travel dirt and weariness slid into the silky, lavender-laced liquid, she thought of the women back in the mountain village and felt guilty. When the young, ebony-skinned couple had carried hot water from the kitchen, she'd felt guilty. And when Emma told her that the middle-aged woman named Nettie would be her personal servant, she felt guilty.

Back at the village, Lillian had explained that all the former slaves working on the plantation were there by choice. When Marcus had started work on the property, he had bought sixteen captives and set them free. He then offered them paid positions on the plantation, along with decent housing and working conditions, as well as an education. Their clothes were well tailored, their shoes well made.

Most had decided to stay, and those who hadn't stayed had soon returned. The result had been a well-organized, prosperous cotton plantation.

Snowbird slid a little farther down into the sudsy water, leaned her head back against the top of the iron, claw-foot tub, and closed her eyes. Perhaps that was why most of the employees she'd encountered since arriving had a positive attitude and a genuine smile on their lips. They knew their master gave them the respect all of God's creations deserved. Respect many of their people had been denied.

Respect the Cherokee had been denied.

Hate and anger chipped away at Snowbird's wall of peace. She released a dejected sigh. *It's me again, Lord,* she silently prayed. *You know how grateful I am that You never tire of hearing from me.* A soft smile curved her lips. *I need Your help right now and in the days to come. I didn't realize coming here would remind me so much of the removal and all that my people have lost. Help me focus on why I am here—to help Marcus—and not on my own past tragedies. Remind me where You brought me from and how far I have come.*

The hate and anger dissipated only to be replaced by another demon. Fear. Fear of seeing Marcus again, fear of his continued rejection, fear of getting hurt again.

But fear, she reminded herself, wasn't of God. So she continued her prayer. *Give me the right words to say to Marcus. Show me how to help him even if he doesn't want me to. Give me the strength to stand firm even in the face of his rejection.*

A swift knock followed by a quick, "Miz Walker?" startled Snowbird. Her head snapped up and her body jerked, sloshing a few drops of the precious scented water on the floor.

Before she could answer, the bedroom door swung open and in breezed the tall and lanky Nettie bearing an armful of towels and a freshly ironed, peach-colored dress.

Nettie plopped the towels on the foot of the four-poster bed covered with its dainty flowered spread, then held up the gown for Snowbird's inspection. "This was Miss Lillian's, but she never wore it," Nettie said like a proud mother. "She was too busy with her book-learning to attend many tea parties. Judging by your size, it only needed a little hem. Ginny took care of that for you." Arranging the elegant garment over the bed, she kept rambling as though talking half to herself and half to Snowbird. "May need a tuck or two in the waist, but we can take care of that later."

"It's beautiful. But should I be wearing my daughter-in-law's clothes without her permission?"

With a graceful black hand, Nettie waved Snowbird's statement away. "Miss Emma gives permission, and so do I." As Nettie straightened and faced the tub, a trace of sadness floated into her ebony eyes. "Since the colonel's been sick, Miss Emma's and my opinion seem to be the only ones that matter as far as running this house is concerned. The colonel, he just has no say-so about anything anymore."

She strolled to the window, which looked out over the distant cotton fields and orchards. "Used to be when he was home, he'd snap out all kinds of instruction about how to run this place." She glanced back at Snowbird, a smile of remembrance playing with the corners of her generous mouth. "Of course, we'd all pretend to listen, make him believe we had a hard time managing the plantation without him while he was away on duty."

Her gaze dropped to the floor while a few seconds passed. When she looked back at Snowbird, she added, "It's a pride thing with men, you know? They like to think they're in control and taking care of things. And letting him think he was doing so, even for those little spaces of time he was here, was our way of showing him how much we love him. After all, he's always been the heart and soul of this place. Things just seem to come more to life whenever he's around." A sad sigh slipped past Nettie's lips. "At least, they used to."

She turned her attention back to the world beyond the window. "The colonel, he's a fine man, that one. If he could just let go of some of that stubborn pride. Then maybe he wouldn't feel so useless. He'd see how much we really do need him."

Nettie scooped up Snowbird's dirty traveling dress from where Snowbird had folded it across a high-back chair and tossed it into a laundry basket along with Snowbird's undergarments. "Sallie will wash these up for you, iron out all those traveling wrinkles." Her lingering sadness was veiled by a proud smile. "She's my daughter."

Pulling a towel from the stack on the bed, Nettie shook out the folds and shuffled over to the bathtub. She held up the towel for Snowbird to step into.

Snowbird, however, sank deeper into the suds. "Thank you, but I prefer to dress myself." She hadn't meant to sound so blunt; the words just came out that way.

Nettie peeked around the towel, her gaze falling to Snowbird's chest, just below her neck. Snowbird resisted the urge to raise her hand to her throat.

"I understand." Nettie folded the towel and laid it across a low mahogany table next to the tub. "Always did appreciate modesty myself."

With that, she turned and quietly left the room.

Snowbird leaned her head back and stared at the soft yellow ceiling where the yawning shades of late afternoon stretched into the shadowed corners.

She gave serious thought to what Nettie had said about Marcus, his place at the plantation, and his relationship with the people. Perhaps he really did belong here among these people, at the home he'd built for his family and those who'd helped him foster it into a successful cotton operation.

And perhaps her place was here with him instead of his place being with her. Perhaps this is what God had been planning for them all along.

But had it taken this tragedy for her to see that?

"No!" she rasped. Guilt smothered her. Surely God didn't allow Marcus to get shot and lose his arm in order to force her to the plantation. She couldn't bear the thought of being the reason for his accident.

She squeezed her eyes shut, and a stinging tear slipped down her face. "No, God, please don't let that be the reason. I couldn't bear it."

Pinpoints of memory flashed through her mind. Marcus coming to tell her Emily was alive. Marcus leaving with the children to take them to their mother. Marcus coming back for her. She released a sigh of relief. Even if she had agreed to go with him to his home, he would have come back to the village after delivering the twins to their mother.

He would have come back for Snowbird regardless.

God's wonderful peace washed over her, calming her with the knowledge that the accident was just that: a horrible accident that would have happened anyway, and He'd redeem the tragedy in His own time.

The water was beginning to chill, and Snowbird accepted the fact that she'd have to leave the silky dream before long. Then she'd have to face Marcus.

Once again, her mind lingered on the things Nettie had said about how much Marcus was needed. *Well*, Snowbird mused, *the people who worked on the plantation aren't the only ones who need him.*

She did, too. She needed him, his love, and his acceptance now more than ever.

But how was she going to convince him of that?

&

"Are you certain he doesn't know Billy and I are here yet?" Snowbird asked Emma some two hours later while the older woman plaited Snowbird's still-damp hair.

Snowbird was fed, rested, and clean for the first time in almost two months. Too bad the uneasiness in her stomach wasn't as simple to wash away as the dirt had been.

"Quite certain, dear," Emma said, handing Snowbird a peach ribbon she'd fished from the top drawer of the dressing-room vanity. "His bedroom window faces the north side of the estate, just as yours does. He rarely knows who's coming or going, and he rarely cares."

The older woman's unconscious remark threw a cold splash of reality in Snowbird's face. Her hands stilled on the barely tied ribbon.

Emma must have realized how thoughtless her slip-of-the-tongue must have sounded, for she met Snowbird's reflection in the oval mirror with chagrin. "Oh, dear, I'm sorry." She laid a hand on Snowbird's shoulder. "I didn't mean that he wouldn't care that you're here."

Snowbird methodically folded her hands on her lap. "We both know he will most likely resent my coming."

"At first, perhaps. But I know you can reach him, Snowbird."

Snowbird shook her head. "I'm not a miracle worker, Emma. Far from it. All I can do is try. This rest is up to him. . .and God."

Emma squeezed Snowbird's shoulder. "You love him

enough to come here knowing he'll most likely resent your presence at first. And he loves you enough to let you go before risking becoming a burden to you. I've got to believe there's a miracle in that."

twelve

Balancing the food-laden tray between her hip and left hand, Snowbird knocked on the tall mahogany door.

"Come in," came a gruff, gritty greeting from the other side. The voice was the same as she remembered but not the tone. Hope was missing.

On the wings of a silent prayer, she turned the brass knob, opened the door, and stepped inside a dungeon. At least it felt like one. Her nostrils filled with heavy, stale air, the kind that stayed locked up in an abandoned cellar for a long, long time.

The room was spacious but dim, lit only by the waning light of day. He stood with his back to her, a dark silhouette against the light and life of the world outside.

He angled his head and paused, as though he sensed something. Snowbird expected him to twist around and look at her. Her grip tightened on the tray.

Then, as though thinking better, he focused his attention back out the window. "Just leave it on the table. You can pick up the tray in an hour."

Snowbird walked softly to the round table at the foot of the bed. Quietly, she eased the tray down, then stood, spine straight, and squared off to face Marcus, folding her hands in front of her. "Hello, Marcus."

He whipped around, and Snowbird forced her gaze to remain fixed on his face and not drop to the half-empty sleeve that flopped at his side. For a heartbeat, she thought she caught a glimpse of delight in his shadowed expression. But whatever the sudden burst of light was, it vanished just as quickly into the heavy sadness haunting the depressing room.

"What are you doing here?" he ground out.

Snowbird mentally reflected the hurt his angry tone threw at her. He'd never directed a harsh word toward her. Never. But she understood the anger that came with pain and loss. "I'm here because your sister invited me."

"She had no right—"

"And. . .I'm here because I wanted to come."

He didn't respond.

"Lillian sends her love."

His stony features softened. "How is she?"

"She's doing well. She's adjusted nicely to her new life and motherhood."

"And little Sara?"

Thoughts of her youngest grandchild brought a smile to Snowbird's lips. "She's wonderful. She had just started walking when I left the valley."

"Ethan and Billy?"

"Ethan's doing quite well. So is Billy. He came with me."

Marcus gave a nod of acknowledgment. "He's a fine young man."

"Yes," Snowbird agreed. "He is."

A short silence passed. "I trust you had a safe and uneventful trip."

Snowbird knew he was simply being polite, so she kept her guard up, her spine straight. "We did, thank you."

He looked away for a moment, swallowed with effort, it seemed, and then looked back at her. His expression was a mixture of pain and confusion. "Why are you here, Snowbird?"

From deep inside her, the words she'd needed to say for a long time slipped past her tongue before she could stop them. "I'm here because I love you, Marcus."

His face twisting in denial, he shook his head. "It's too late for us, Snowbird."

Slowly, methodically, she began to close the distance between them. "I don't believe that, Marcus. You didn't feel it was too late a year ago."

"Things have changed. I have changed."

As she rounded the foot of the heavy, four-poster bed, she ran a palm lightly across one of the bed's ornamental posts. "How?"

"What?"

"How have you changed, Marcus?"

"Don't be so callous, Snowbird. It doesn't suit you."

As she stopped two feet in front of him, she noticed his hair had grown far too long. He'd neglected to shave for several days, and he probably hadn't bathed in at least two.

"I wasn't trying to be callous," she said. "I know you lost your arm, and I'm deeply sorry for the pain and despondency it has caused you. But you haven't lost your heart or soul. Nothing can take that from you unless you allow it."

He studied her for a moment; then his features turned stony. "I hope you enjoy your visit."

Then he turned his back to her and stared out the window.

Suddenly overcome by her own need for solitude, Snowbird slipped quietly from the room. By the time she got back to the guest quarters, she was gasping for breath. She thought she'd prepared herself for seeing Marcus without his right arm. But when he'd turned to face her for the first time, his empty shirtsleeve flopping at his side, and glared at her through the hollowed eyes of a stranger, she'd bled inside.

As far as her feelings for him were concerned, his missing limb didn't change anything. But what this tragedy had done to him—destroying the strong, confident, happy man she once had known—tormented her.

She knew what it was like to be emotionally destroyed. She also knew healing could take a long time and was virtually impossible without God.

Right now, it seemed Marcus wanted no one's help, including God's.

Tears began to fall. In the middle of her room, she fell to her knees, wrapped her arms around herself, and began to pray.

❧

Marcus stood staring unseeingly out his bedroom window, the stub of his missing arm resting in his left hand. The last thing he expected, the last thing he wanted, was for Snowbird to show up at his home looking like she'd just stepped out of one of his dreams.

Her lingering scent, soft and untamed with just a hint of lavender, filled his senses. A buried emotion rose and squeezed his chest. It was the first thing other than anger that he'd felt in six months.

He strolled over to the table, looked down at the tray of food, and realized he didn't want it.

Raking his only hand through his disheveled hair, he walked back to the window. As he stared out at the long shadows stretching across his yard, he rubbed the stub of his arm where he once had an elbow. A numbing tingle shot up to his shoulder.

When Snowbird Walker decided to do something, there was no deterring her. And she'd obviously decided to convince him they still had a chance at a happy life together.

Oppression bore down upon him. He obviously had a problem.

❧

"Oh, Miss Snowbird! What in the world you doin'?"

The high, shrill voice surrounded Snowbird like the warning call of a mountain lion just before attack. The cast-iron skillet she was about to place on the wood-burning stove hit the stove top with a clash.

She turned as the short, plump Sadie came waddling around the table. Her salt-and-pepper hair was pulled back tight and twisted into an uncomfortable-looking bun, away from her dark, rounded face. The gingham apron rode high on her rounded belly, the band tucked beneath an ample bosom.

"I'm cooking breakfast," Snowbird replied.

"You're not supposed to be doin' that!" Sadie reached for the pan with a stout hand and brushed Snowbird aside with her commanding presence. "That's what the colonel pays me to do."

"I don't mind helping." In fact, Snowbird preferred to.

"No, ma'am. Nobody cooks in Sadie's kitchen but Sadie." The cook stepped to the side of the informal kitchen table and pulled out a ladder-back oak chair. "Now you just sit down right here, and I'll pour you a cup of coffee."

For the first time in her life, Snowbird did as she was told. Acquiescence felt strange and awkward, like a shoe on the wrong foot.

Sadie poured a steaming dark brew into a delicate china

cup. "How you like your coffee, ma'am?"

Snowbird tipped her head toward the cup Sadie held up. "That's fine."

"No cream or sugar?"

"No, thank you. Just plain coffee will do for me."

"That's me." Sadie set the cup and saucer in front of Snowbird. "Don't want no sweets or cream messing up the taste of a good cup of coffee."

As the cook started to walk away, Snowbird clasped her hand. "When you get the colonel's tray prepared, I'll take it up."

The cook's shoulder dropped in relief. "Yes, ma'am, Miz Walker. Now I'll be glad to let you take over that part of my duties. The colonel, he's just not himself since he lost his arm." Dropping her gaze to the floor, she shook her head. "Breaks my heart to see him that way."

"I know." Snowbird swallowed a rising lump of sorrow and squeezed the cook's hand. "Sadie?" Snowbird waited until she had the cook's attention, then added, "My name is Snowbird."

Sadie's lips split into a broad grin, revealing an even row of amazingly white teeth. "Yes ma'am, Miz Snowbird."

Ten minutes later, Snowbird, with a tray weighted down with fine china, eggs, bacon, biscuits, and peach preserves, knocked on Marcus's door.

"Who is it?"

Snowbird rolled her eyes. He wouldn't have asked had he not known she was standing outside his door instead of the cook. "It's me. Snowbird."

She waited an impatient moment, and when he didn't respond added, "I have your breakfast."

"Set it outside the door."

Snowbird glanced at the small mahogany table standing in the hall next to his bedroom door. It hadn't been there the evening before, but she wasn't surprised. And she was prepared.

She balanced the tray against her hip and fished out of her skirt pocket the key Emma had given her the evening before.

When she opened the door, she slipped the key back into her pocket and breezed into the same picture she'd walked into the day before: Marcus standing with his back to her, staring out the window, breathing dead air. The awakening morning did give the room a little more light. But the sparkling, dew-kissed blanket of life beyond his dull window only made Marcus's limited world seem that much more depressing. How did he get from one day to the next without suffocating?

"I asked you to leave the tray outside," he said without turning around.

Snowbird bristled. This was the man who'd asked her to marry him not once, but thrice. He'd pursued her until she'd given her heart to him for the second time in her life. Now he was trying to push her away. Well, she'd be dead and buried before she allowed his feelings of worthlessness and self-pity to stand between them. They'd been through too much, come too far.

She straightened her shoulders and strengthened her resolve. Marching to the table, she plunked down the tray with enough force that the china rattled and a few drops of coffee sloshed over the edge of the cup. Then she strode to the window opposite the side of the bed where Marcus stood and swept back the gold-colored damask curtain.

A million particles of dust attacked her face and raced

to her lungs. A couple of hearty sneezes cleared them out. Quickly recovering, she tucked her fingers into the grooves on the bottom of the window frame and pulled. It wouldn't open. With the heels of her hands, she pushed up on the top frame of the bottom window. The wood creaked but still didn't give.

She felt Marcus looking at her out of the corner of his eye. She sensed his amusement at her futile efforts.

Pursing her lips, she pushed. And pushed again. Finally, on the forth shove, the dirty-paned window gave way, and the wooden frame scraped up its tracks. The morning air was like a soothing balm to her dusty skin. She breathed in deep the fresh scent of earth and dew that flowed through the opening.

"What are you trying to do?" Marcus asked.

Dusting off her hands by brushing one against the other, she squared off to face him. He was looking at her like she'd lost her good sense.

"I'm letting some much-needed fresh air into this room."

"I don't recall giving you permission."

"I don't recall asking for your permission." In one swift movement, she jerked the gold-colored comforter off his unmade bed, rolled it up, and tossed it onto the seat of a nearby chair.

Marcus's brow creased. "Have you gone mad?"

Without so much as a pause in her movements, she started peeling the linens off his bed. "I was about to ask you the same thing. Honestly, Marcus, I never thought I'd see you lock yourself away like this, wallowing in self-pity like a spoiled child who's just been scolded and sent to his room."

He did a quarter turn so that his whole body faced her. "I beg your pardon?"

"You heard me." She shook a pillow from its pillowcase.

He didn't respond, just stood there, mouth hanging open like whatever he wanted to say next was lodged somewhere in his throat.

She yanked the bottom sheet from the mattress and, while she bundled it up, chanced meeting his gaze head-on. He looked both baffled and angry. Very angry. She was grateful the bed stood between them.

Gathering the bundled sheet against her chest, she said, "I won't let you do this to yourself, Marcus. You've got too much of life ahead of you, too much left to give."

"I have nothing left to give."

"You're lying to yourself. You've got plenty left to give."

His jaw clenched. His nostrils flared. With his left hand, he pulled up his right shirtsleeve to reveal the discolored blunt end of his upper arm. "What can I do with this?"

She kept her gaze fixed on his, her way of refusing to acknowledge what he viewed as a crippling handicap. "You've got a brilliant mind, Marcus. Why don't you use it to figure out what you can do?"

Shaking his head, he pushed his sleeve back down. "You have no idea what's it's like to be maimed."

And he had no idea what he was talking about, so she decided to show him. Grinding her teeth together, she threw the crumpled sheet back down on the mattress. With calculated steps, she walked around the bed, holding his gaze with steadfast determination. When she'd narrowed the distance between them to two feet, she stopped. Reaching up, she began unfastening the top button of her high collar.

His angry expression turned to one of shock and confusion. "What on earth are you doing?"

She unbuttoned the second button.

"Stop it!" Raising his only hand, he grasped one of her wrists.

She knocked his hand away and unbuttoned a third button, then the fourth, stopping halfway between her neck and chest. Then, while he stared at her like a stunned adolescent, she opened the collar of her dress to reveal a portion of skin marked by the scars three drunken white men had carved into her body almost nineteen years ago.

❧

Marcus stared at her once satin-smooth skin now marred by unsightly puckered scars branded into her chest.

His stomach churned. For the first time since his accident, he forgot himself and his ailment. He forgot about everything but the woman standing before him.

"Repulsive, aren't they?" came Snowbird's voice. Words laced with acrimony.

He lifted his gaze to eyes full of a myriad of tangled emotions: pain, anger, shame, and yes, even pride. She had survived the worst thing a woman could survive and borne the scars every day as reminders of it. Yet she had somehow risen above it and became a leader to her people, a wise mother to her children, a gifted medicinal healer, a woman cherished by many, including himself.

"Those aren't the only ones," she said. "There are others on my stomach. . .my back. . . ."

She paused, leaving words unsaid. Turning her back to him, she started refastening her dress. "I was going to say yes," she tossed back over her shoulder.

He didn't ask what she was referring to. He knew.

Once she had fastened the last button, she once again faced

him. "When you returned to the valley, I was going to accept your proposal. Of course, I wondered how you'd react to the scars the first time you saw them. But I knew if you sincerely loved me—and I believe you do—it wouldn't matter. It wouldn't change things between us."

He swallowed the tears burning the back of his throat and resisted the need to reach up and touch her face. She'd been through too much. He'd not place another hardship on her, even if, out of some sense of loyalty she felt she owed him. He couldn't let her tie herself to a cripple. She deserved better. And with him out of the way, she'd find it.

"Suppose I had made it back to the valley," he said, "and when you showed me the scars, I began to pity you."

"You wouldn't have, Marcus." Her voice was soft and confident, her dark eyes softer. "You may feel anger toward the men who did this to me and guilt that you couldn't prevent it. But you'd never pity me. I wouldn't allow it."

She was right. She would never allow anyone to pity her. She was too strong. Stronger, obviously, than he. Looking straight at her, he said, "And I'll not allow you to feel sorry for me."

"Oh, Marcus, I don't feel sorry for you."

He didn't believe her, even though her unveiled expression told him she was telling the truth.

Shoulders dropping as she released a weary sigh, she added, "Pity doesn't benefit anyone, Marcus. Especially the one feeling sorry for himself."

A jolt of anger shot through him like a burning arrow. He scowled at her, which didn't seem to deter her a bit.

She clasped her hands in front of her, a true lady all poised and proper. Yet he knew what a headstrong and untamed spirit lay just beneath that polished demeanor.

"You've been dealt a devastating blow," she added. "But God obviously isn't through with you yet, is He? Or you wouldn't still be here. Now, you can stay up here in this depressing room, closed off from those who love and care about you, or you can find a way to turn this tragedy into a triumph."

Turning her attention to the bed, she gathered up the stale bedding. "I'll see that fresh linens are put back on your bed as soon as I figure out where they are."

Before stepping through the door, she turned back to him. "I'll also see you have a lunch tray. But tonight, dinner will be at six in the dining room. I'll have Sadie set your place. I'll also see you have a fresh suit to wear."

Without giving him a chance to argue, she breezed through the door, closing it with a soft and deliberate *click*.

All Marcus could do for a long time was stare at the space she'd left empty. He wanted to be angry with her. She'd come into his home without his consent or knowledge and imposed herself upon his sanctuary of solitude that no one else dared enter. She was bossy, headstrong, and, it seemed, had blown in here like a strong summer storm and taken charge like she was mistress of the house.

Exactly what he'd desperately longed for less than a year ago. Exactly what he could now only dream of.

He rubbed the stub that was once his right elbow, running his fingers across the rough edges of the scar. The wound had not only left him maimed and disfigured on the outside but also angry and bitter on the inside. He didn't want to live among the living, didn't want people staring at him, asking questions so he would have to relive the harrowing experience. He didn't want anyone's pity. Especially Snowbird's.

He sat down on the bare mattress and ran the fingers of his awkward left hand through his disheveled hair. He envied Snowbird. She was a woman full of willpower, courage, and fortitude. How could one person endure so much and carry on? How could one mortal being be so strong?

Gazing out the window, he drew in a deep breath and followed up with a forlorn sigh. He had once thought himself a strong man. He was trained to be a soldier and protector. His greatest desire had been to shield the woman he loved from any more pain and danger. But in an instant, a man who thought he could conquer any battle had been taken down. And no matter how hard he tried, he couldn't claw his way out of the deep, dark hole he had fallen into. Couldn't rise above the feeling of hopelessness. Couldn't defeat the paralyzing feelings of uselessness that tormented his mind.

He still believed in God, but where was He in all this? Marcus had tried to pray, but it seemed no one listened. No one cared.

Exhaustion washed through him, so he did the only thing he knew would give his troubled spirit a few hours' reprieve. He curled up on the bare mattress and went to sleep.

thirteen

What do you think we should do?" Emma wanted to know.

She and Frederick sat across from Snowbird and Billy at the large mahogany dining room table laden with food. The chair at the head of the table was vacant.

Snowbird spread her linen napkin across her lap. "It's six o'clock. I think we should eat."

"But what about Marcus?" Emma's voice was timid with concern.

So was Snowbird's mind, but she didn't want anyone else to sense it. "I told him dinner would be at six. He apparently decided not to join us."

Emma cast an anxious glance toward the heavy double doors marking the dining room entrance. "Well. . .I suppose I can take a tray up to him once we've finished eating."

"I don't think that would be a good idea."

"Why not?"

"Because as long as we cater to him, he'll have no reason to come out of that dungeon."

"But—"

Frederick patted his wife's hand. "Trust Snowbird, dear. She only has Marcus's best interests at heart."

❧

After dinner, Snowbird stopped by Marcus's room to tell him breakfast would be at seven the following morning.

At 7:05 a.m., his seat at the table was still vacant.

After the morning meal, Snowbird once again stopped by Marcus's room to tell him lunch would be served at noon. His place remained empty during that meal, also.

Snowbird had a feeling that the evening would be different. After all, a man couldn't ignore the gnawing teeth of hunger too long.

At precisely 6:00 p.m., Marcus walked into the dining room. Without a word, not even so much as a greeting, he sat down at the head of the table. After Frederick blessed the food, Marcus ate, self-consciously, with his left hand. Snowbird hoped he wouldn't notice she'd had the cook prepare foods that didn't require cutting or the use of both hands.

He kept his head down, wiped his chin often, and responded in monosyllabic words only when spoken to.

The instant he finished eating, he pushed his chair away from the table and returned to his room.

This routine continued for the morning and evening meals for the next seven days. Snowbird delivered a tray to his room for the noon meal.

She always spoke to Marcus but was seldom spoken to. She opened windows, dusted furniture, freshened his wardrobe, and put on a cheerful veneer in the presence of a man who had withdrawn into a dark, distant existence.

But inside, Snowbird wept.

ॐ

Eight days later, Snowbird followed Marcus from the dining room after the breakfast meal. "Marcus?"

He paused halfway up the carpeted stairs and turned to look at her where she stood at the bottom of the steps.

"Would you like to go riding with me today?" she asked. "I thought I'd visit the cotton fields."

"No, thank you." He turned and trudged up the stairs to his room.

This routine continued for the next seven days.

❧

"Marcus?"

Marcus stopped halfway up the stairs, turned, and looked down at Snowbird. Something sharp and swift kicked him in the chest. The blow was harder than the one he'd experienced yesterday, which was harder than the day before. He couldn't control his reaction to her, no matter how hard he tried. He couldn't deny she was beginning to chip away at the black ice that had frozen his soul.

"Would you like to go riding with me today?" she asked, her face just as full of anticipation as it had been every day for the last seven days.

"You're not going to give up, are you?"

Her answer was a dazzling, dauntless smile.

"If I agree to go today, will you leave me alone for a while?"

"Absolutely not."

He almost smiled. Almost. "I'll be ready at ten."

"I'll have Sadie pack us some lunch." With that, she flitted away like an exotic butterfly.

❧

How on earth was he going to manage this without falling on his backside and making a spectacle of himself? Chester, his chestnut-colored gelding, nosed Marcus's arm in greeting. Marcus ran his hand down the horse's glistening neck and felt the power of well-toned muscles. The horse had not been neglected, thanks to his overseer, Hank.

"Yes, old boy," Marcus murmured, "I've missed you, too." To himself he added, *I just don't know how I'm going to mount you and hold on to my dignity.*

The sun warmed his back. A faint breeze whispered across his face and rippled the animal's dark mane. Marcus breathed in deep and smelled horse, leather, and the white clover dotting the green hillsides. He smelled. . .life.

He gazed out over the rolling land adorned with dogwoods, tulip poplars, oaks, and a vast variety of other native hardwoods. Not so long ago, he'd thought he'd one day retire from the military and spend his days among the gardens and orchards of the plantation. He'd always had an interest in watching things grow. Seeing new life break forth from the earth excited him during his times at home. He found pleasure in hearing about one year's crop doing better than the previous year's.

However, it wasn't quite the life he'd dreamed of as a boy back in Spring Place. Then, his dreams consisted to two things only: being a soldier and marrying Snowbird.

He'd accomplished his first dream with ease. But a cruel lie told by his own father had banished all hopes of the life he'd planned with Snowbird.

Thinking she was dead had left him heartbroken and barren. He'd never forgotten her or how he'd loved her with every breath he breathed. Yet he'd somehow gone on with his life. He'd survived.

When he later met Sara, his adopted daughter's mother, he settled into the role of husband and father. He bought a piece of land, built a home for his new family, and fell easily into a nice, predictable life. He set goals, planned his future, meticulously structured his life on a scale he could control.

Even after Sara had died and he was weighed down with grief, he knew life would somehow go on. He would continue being a soldier until he was forced to retire; then he would come home to the nice, quiet life of a farmer as he'd planned. There was simply something about having your own place carved out in the world—a place waiting to welcome you with open arms when the blazing fire of life began to settle into a calm, steady flame.

Then, like the unexpected storm slips up on a ship, Snowbird had come back into his life and knocked him off course. All at once, property and crops and predictability didn't mean so much anymore. It no longer mattered which direction his life was headed, as long as he was headed in that direction with her.

And even though his well-laid plans had changed, he'd still had a sense of determination. He'd had to redraft the road map of his life, but he'd still had goals. And he'd known exactly what he wanted.

Then in the flash of a musket, everything changed. A case of mistaken identity had taken every hope and dream within Marcus's steady grasp and severed it right along with his arm.

He no longer had any sense of direction in life. He just existed from one droning day to the next, wondering why God had allowed him to live. He was just a body, an empty vessel taking up space. He had no goal. He had no purpose.

The soft sound of foot and hoof meeting the earth punctured his despondent thoughts. He glanced back over his shoulder to see his trusted overseer, Hank, ambling out of the stables leading Molly, the gentle brown-and-white painted mare Snowbird would be riding.

"I say it once, and I say it again," the tall black man said, "it sure is good to see you out and about on this fine, wonderful day." Little beads of sweat glistened on his forehead. A wide grin etched crow's-feet at the corners of his black eyes. A wide-brimmed straw hat sat atop his balding head.

Marcus couldn't disagree with Hank. The colonel had forgotten how good it felt to work up a good, laborious sweat.

And to smile. He'd forgotten what it felt like to smile. "Thank you, Hank. And thank you for getting Chester and Molly saddled up and ready to go."

"You're welcome, sir." Hank turned his attention toward the house. "My, my. That Miss Snowbird is one fine lady. And almos' as pretty as my Nettie on our weddin' day."

Marcus twisted around, and his breath hitched in his chest. His palms broke out in a cold sweat. Snowbird strolled across the lawn, a wide-brimmed straw hat secured by a green ribbon sat atop her head. She wore a simple green dress that swirled around her delicate ankles with each casual step she took. A picnic satchel dangled from her right hand.

Hank wrapped the mare's reins around the hitching post and took off in an easy trot to meet Snowbird. "Here, Miss Snowbird, let me take that for you."

She greeted him with a gracious smile. Passing him the satchel, she then slipped a small hand into the crook of Hank's arm.

Watching the exchange, Marcus blinked, then furrowed his brow in enlightening thought. Snowbird was in her element, he realized. She was refined, well-educated—as were her children—and she knew what it took to manage a plantation.

She'd lived this life once and had watched it crumble chip by sorrowful chip around her feet. She had been abused by his government, assaulted and scarred by three white men, and a fugitive living in the Appalachian wilderness for two years to escape removal to the West.

She'd been knocked down by life's tragedies time and again. Yet she was still standing, prouder and stronger than ever.

How did she do it?

"I hope I haven't kept you gentlemen waiting too long," she said as she stopped beside Molly.

"No, ma'am," Hank replied. "Not at all."

Hank slung the satchel across the back of Molly's saddle, securing it in the process, then assisted Snowbird while she mounted.

He turned to Marcus. "You need some help, sir?"

Probably, Marcus said to himself. Aloud, he added, "No, thank you."

"Alright, then. You young folks have a nice day." With a tip of his hat, the cheerful overseer turned and sauntered back into the stable.

Marcus glanced at Snowbird, who appeared to be gazing off into the distance. In reality, he knew she was giving him time to mount without feeling scrutinized by another.

He looped the reins over the horse's head and grasped the horn of the saddle. It felt strange and awkward standing there, wanting to reach for the back of the saddle with a hand that wasn't there.

When he lifted his booted left foot to the stirrup, his leg and back muscles burned with resistance. Odd, how a few months of idleness could undo years of hard work and training.

Defeat stole the small measure of courage he'd summoned in order to even agree to accompanying Snowbird on the ride to start with. "I don't know if I can do this."

Without turning to look at him, she replied, "I think you can, Marcus. God's grace is sufficient."

Her words rekindled that dying ember of courage somewhere deep inside Marcus. He took two deep, fortifying breaths and whispered a silent prayer. *God, help me.* Grasping the saddle horn with his hand once more, he slipped his left foot in the stirrup and pushed off the ground with his right foot. Once settled, he noticed he felt winded and jerky. The once-effortless task had made Marcus feel clumsy and demanded his full focus and concentration. But he'd made it. And when Snowbird turned to smile at him, he felt his face flush and ducked his head like a gangly adolescent with a crush on his beautiful teacher.

They rode over a grassy hill, where the seemingly endless cotton fields lay in full lacy-white blooms. At least a dozen laborers worked at tilling the ground and checking plants for disease.

But Marcus noticed one worker who didn't quite fit in. His shiny, black, shoulder-length hair held in place by a red bandanna was straight, not curly, and his skin wasn't nearly as dark as the others'.

Marcus gave Chester's rein a gentle tug. The gelding eased to a stop. "What's Billy doing in the field?"

Snowbird eased her mount to a stop. "Billy isn't content unless he's doing something productive."

"But he's my guest."

Snowbird cut a glance Marcus's way.

He knew exactly what she was thinking. Her first day at the plantation, he'd made it clear he'd not been the one who'd extended the invitation to her—or Billy. Guilt pricked his conscience. How could he have treated her with such disrespect? "You know what I mean," he said. "He's a guest here regardless of who invited him."

"Doesn't matter. Billy always has to be doing." Pride blanketed her expression as she studied her son. "He's a restless soul."

"Colonel! Colonel!"

Three children, two boys ages four and seven and a girl around age five, if Marcus's memory served him correctly, practically skidded to a halt next to his right heel. The threesome didn't say anything else, just stood, looking at Marcus with an expression of anticipation.

He knew what the children wanted, what they'd come to expect. In the past, whenever he was home and would visit the cotton fields, he'd bring treats for the children. This time, as he readied himself for his outing with Snowbird, all he could think about was how hard getting through the day would be. The children of his loyal employees hadn't even entered his mind until he'd seen the three youngsters running across the field to greet him.

"Ike, Jake, Elizabeth," he greeted the children by name. "I'm terribly sorry, but—"

"But Colonel Gunter didn't have any fresh blueberries for the muffins this morning," came Snowbird's cheerful voice. "I'm afraid you'll have to settle for teacakes." The children and Marcus watched as she dug a small sack out of the saddlebag and held it out to Marcus.

Sadie, his trusted cook, had obviously remembered his cherished ritual and shared it with Snowbird.

He wrapped Chester's reins around the saddle horn and, with a grateful nod to Snowbird, reached for the sack. Passing the treats down to the girl standing in the middle of the trio, he said, "Here you go, Elizabeth. I'll let you be in charge of passing out the teacakes. I know you'll see everyone gets their fair share."

Seeming in awe, the wide-eyed girl stared at the cloth sack she held in her hands as if she'd just been given a box of priceless jewels to pass out among her friends. "Thank you, Colonel."

"Thank you, Colonel," the two boys echoed. Then the children ran across the field to share their sweets with the workers.

Marcus took a moment to study Snowbird, who watched the children dig the treats from the bag. Her eyes sparkled with delight. Her lips tipped softly. She looked content, happy—as if she belonged there.

If only. . .

As though sensing his thoughts, she angled her head, meeting his gaze. "What is it? Do I have something on my face?"

Yes, he wanted to say. *You have the most beautiful eyes—a man could get lost in them. You have the most enchanting nose, and the softest lips in the world.*

"No," he said out loud. "Thank you so much for remembering the treats."

"Don't thank me. Thank Sadie. She's the one who knew what to do."

"Please thank her for me when we get back to the house."

"Now, Colonel, I think Sadie would love to hear you thank her yourself. Surely you can manage that on your way back to your room."

He could have taken her remark as accusatory and been offended, but he didn't. He knew Snowbird well enough by now to know she spoke the truth to be honest, not cruel or sarcastic.

"All right," he agreed, "I will."

He noticed a hint of surprise in Snowbird's eyes. Then she smiled, and he sensed she was pleased with his efforts to step out of his dark world, where he felt safe and shielded from scrutinizing and sympathetic eyes.

He felt his soul wanting to reach out to her, to open up his heart and accept the love and life she was offering. But he reminded himself that wasn't how their relationship was supposed to go. He was supposed to continue on in his misery until she gave up on him and went back to her people and her former life where she belonged.

Snowbird reached down and closed the open flap of her saddlebag. "Sadie told me about the perfect picnic spot, with a huge white oak for shade and the sound of running water."

"I'd say Sadie knows what she's talking about. Let's go." Unwinding the reins from the saddle horn, he urged Chester forward at a leisurely pace.

The place Sadie had suggested for Marcus and Snowbird's lunch was one of Marcus's favorite places on the plantation. He and Sara had picnicked there twice. He would have taken her much more often, but she detested outdoor activity, especially eating on the ground among various offspring of Mother Nature. But he'd continue to come. In the past when he'd take leave from his military duties, he'd found nothing more rejuvenating to his soul than the peace and solitude he found by the river that ran through the west end of his property.

As he and Snowbird topped the rolling knoll, he could hear the gurgle of the stream. A meadow of wildflowers, blankets of lavender, gold, and green, rippled in the whisper of a breeze. Just a few feet from the river's edge stood an aged oak, her massive arms stretched out in welcome with the promise of shelter from the approaching midday sun.

Snowbird remained silent until they slowed their horses to a stop beneath the oak's sweeping canopy. "This is a beautiful place, Marcus. So peaceful."

"Thank you," he replied, and until that moment, he hadn't realized just how much he'd missed coming here.

He dismounted. Snowbird, who appeared to be engrossed by the dancing water in the stream, did not.

He contemplated his next move. A gentleman with two good arms would offer to lift her down. What would one with only one arm do?

He took one step, then two, and stopped on the left side of her horse. "Snowbird?"

She turned her head and looked down at him, smiled a soft, trusting smile, and reached down her hand.

His chest tightened, and his gaze fell to the outstretched palm. He didn't want this, he reminded himself. He didn't need someone depending on him for anything—not even helping her off her horse. He lifted his eyes back up to Snowbird, and the beauty born of trust overwhelmed him. Humbled him. The pressure in his chest rose to include an ache in his throat.

He forced himself to swallow and wet his lips. "Snowbird, I don't think I can do this."

"I think—"

He shook his head, cutting her off.

She waited a few contemplative seconds. "Marcus." Her voice held a slight lecturing tone. "I know your life has changed. You can't do things like you once did. You have to make adjustments. I also know a person can do anything if he wants to badly enough." A challenging glint sparked in her eyes. "I guess the question to answer at the moment is, 'How badly do you want to help me down?'"

A defeated sigh released some of the tightness in his chest. He couldn't figure out if he was angry at the sly way she had of pushing him into things he never intended doing, or if he was grateful she had badgered him into venturing out on such a lovely, sun-kissed day.

"I'm not asking you to move a mountain," she said, interrupting the debate teeter-tottering inside his head. "Just a hand will do."

Warily, he raised his hand.

She didn't take it. Instead, she leaned down, placed a hand on each of his shoulders, and slid off the mare.

He reflexively reached up, placed his left hand beneath her right arm and the end of his half arm beneath her left arm. Effortlessly, like a feather floating on a breeze, she landed softly on her feet.

And there they stood, face-to-face, arms embracing each other.

The scent of wild trees and lilac teased his senses almost to the point of intoxication. Her soft, warm breath caressed his face. How could he be around her and keep denying his love for her?

Another thought penetrated his waning resistance. How could he ask her to tie herself to him when his life seemed so unclear and uncertain?

"Snowbird," he heard himself say. "We can't do this."

Her eyes stretched wide in obvious surprise. Pushing him

away, she turned her back to him, but not before he caught a glimpse of pain rising in her face.

"I'm sorry, Marcus," she said, "I didn't mean. . .it wasn't my intention. . ."

Confusion marred his forehead, then dawning realization smoothed it. She thought that he thought she was being coquettish. What he'd actually meant was it wasn't right she sacrifice her life with her people for a crippled, broken man. She deserved to be happy—and free.

Taking a step toward her, he reached out. "No, Snowbird, you misunderstood."

She whipped back around, wide eyes pooled with tears and hurt. And in that single defining moment, he knew what he had to do. He dropped his hand for fear contact would weaken his resolve to keep himself distanced from her.

She blinked away the moisture in her eyes. "I did?"

"Yes, you did. I meant it's not right for you to give up everything you love and hold dear to come here and take care of me."

"But I've not given up everything I love, Marcus. When are you going to accept that I'm here because I want to be?"

He shook his head. "No, you're not. You're here because my sister wrote you and begged you to come. You came because that's who you are. A helper and a healer. You'd not turn anyone away."

"You give me too much credit. I'd not leave my family and my life for just any cause. It would have to be one dear to my heart, one I believe in." She stepped closer, raising a hand to his cheek.

He almost came undone.

"I believe in you, Marcus," she added. "Whether you believe

in yourself or not, I believe in you with all my heart."

He knew that. He also knew she would stay for as long as she thought he needed her, and within that knowledge lay the key to her freedom.

fourteen

Holding up a hand mirror, Snowbird turned her back to the vanity mirror to check the bow she'd fastened in her hair. She'd abandoned her habitual single braid for a more fashionable style, fastening the top half of her hair back and allowing her thick, glossy mane to hang loose down her back. She'd also taken extra care in choosing the yellow day dress she now wore.

Was it vanity making her act like a belle, or a desire to please the man she loved? Most definitely a desire to please the man she loved, she decided as she patted the hair above one ear into place. She wanted to show him she could fit into his world. She wanted to be ready to accompany him when he was ready to step back into the life he knew before his accident.

Tilting her chin, she adjusted the high collar of her dress. The picnic had gone well yesterday, although Marcus had seemed a bit distant once they'd cleared up their misunderstanding of each other's thoughts after he'd helped off her horse. But he was just nervous, she told herself. After all, he'd taken a big step by even venturing outside the house. Progress would take time.

Taking one last look in the mirror, she headed for the door and tried to quell the uneasiness nagging at the back of her mind, hinting something was about to change.

She found Sadie in the kitchen, working at the stove and

humming a happy tune. "Good morning, Sadie."

The cook turned, a wide smile spread across her broad face. "Why, good morning, Miz Snowbird. My, don't you look extra pretty this mornin'."

"Thank you. And you seem to be in extra good spirits today."

"Yes, ma'am, I am. The colonel, why he come down here before daylight this mornin', jes' like he used to do, wantin' his breakfast so he could get about his day."

It was then Snowbird noticed a plate with a half-eaten biscuit and a half-empty cup of coffee on the table. "Where is he now?"

"He done gone out to check on the men in the field." With a laugh that shook both belly and bosom, Sadie dished a pan of eggs onto a plate. "Shore does ol' Sadie's heart good to see the colonel acting like his ol' self."

Snowbird didn't know what to think. Of course, she'd expected progress, prayed for it. But not so much so soon. What did it mean?

"Yes, dat was my reaction, too. When he come down here an' ordered up a full-course breakfast, I couldn't believe it at first. But there he was, just as big as life itself."

"That's wonderful, Sadie." Snowbird reached for the cup of coffee the cook offered her. "Just wonderful."

But was it? Depression wasn't something someone overcame in a single day. She glanced out the window. What should she do? Go and find Marcus, or leave him to his business?

After breakfast, she asked Hank to saddle Molly and then rode out to the cotton fields. She stopped when she topped the hill, remaining in the shadow of an old oak tree. The scene was pretty much the same as the day before, but Marcus walked among the workers, stopping occasionally to inspect the plants and laugh at something one of the men said. Her gaze found Billy. He worked steadily, seemingly unaffected by the man whose presence evoked an air of celebration.

As though sensing her presence, Billy glanced her way for a fleeting moment, then went right on working.

Snowbird chewed on her lower lip, considering whether to go on down to the field or return to the house. In the end, she decided to leave the seemingly jovial Marcus and return to the house. Today appeared to be a good day, but who knew what tomorrow would be?

But tomorrow was no different. Or the next day. Or the next. Marcus, it seemed, had made a full and complete recovery. He'd returned to the world of the living and included everyone at the plantation in his day-to-day activities.

Everyone. . .except Snowbird.

One month later, it was obvious he no longer needed her.

૨ઐ

At the sound of the soft knock on his study door, Marcus looked up from the ledger he was studying. "Come in."

The door opened just enough for Snowbird to slip inside. "May I speak with you a minute?"

He steadied his breathing but was unable to calm his erratic heartbeat. "Of course."

She closed the door and moved across the floor like an angel. Stopping in front of his desk, she folded her hands in front of her.

"Please, sit down." He motioned to the chair next to her.

"Thank you, but I can't stay. I just came to tell you that Billy and I will be leaving tomorrow morning."

Something punched him in the chest with such force

he couldn't breathe for a full five seconds. *This is what you wanted*, he reminded himself. *This is what you set out to accomplish when you decided to act like you no longer needed her.* But he hadn't expected her announcement to deliver such an unsettling blow. After all, he'd had a month to prepare himself for this moment.

"Must you go so soon?" he heard himself say.

"We need to get back to the village before bad weather sets in."

"I see. I'll have Mr. Nelms accompany you."

"That won't be necessary. Billy and I will be fine traveling alone."

"I insist. There's still a lot of unrest over the removal. It'll be safer traveling under the guise of a family of three."

She responded with a simple nod, turned, and started to leave, but stopped halfway to the door and looked back at him. "I'm happy for you, Marcus. You have a wonderful life here."

If she only knew. "Thank you. I'm sure you're anxious to get back to yours."

She held his gaze for a long, painful moment, and he quelled the yearning to ask her to stay.

Her lips turned up in a sad, poignant smile that bespoke remembrances both bitter and sweet. "I have a lot to be thankful for. You've given me two beautiful children and an abundance of precious memories that will remain with me for the rest of my life."

With that, she ducked her head and slipped out the door.

Closing the ledger, Marcus leaned back in his leather chair and stared at the darkening ceiling. He'd done it. He'd finally convinced her he no longer needed her.

Life would go on, he knew. He would survive. Snowbird had taught him that when she waltzed into his life six weeks ago and forced him to crawl out of his self-imposed exile.

But would he continue to live the way she had taught him to?

He laid his hand over his hurting heart. He seriously doubted it. Otherwise, he wouldn't feel like his last candle had just been snuffed out.

Fifteen minutes later, Marcus was still staring at the ceiling, trying to convince himself he'd done the right thing. Then the door to his study opened once again. He leaned forward in his chair, expecting to see Snowbird, hoping she was returning to tell him she'd changed her mind.

Instead, he found Billy strolling casually across the room. He took off his straw hat and set it on the corner of Marcus's desk. Without waiting for permission, the lad eased down in one of the guest chairs in front of Marcus's desk, crossed one ankle on top of the opposite knee, propped his elbows on the chair's arms, and clasped his hands over his stomach. He didn't say a word, just studied Marcus like he was a puzzle with an ill-fitting piece.

Marcus wasn't quite sure how to take Billy's actions. The young Cherokee was a book Marcus hadn't yet figured out how to read and suspected he never would.

"Your mother tells me you're leaving in the morning," Marcus commented, in an effort to start a conversation.

"Yep," Billy replied. "How does that make you feel?"

"It doesn't matter how it makes me feel. What matters is what's best for your mother."

"And how would you know that?"

Marcus didn't like the kid's tone or where the conversation

was headed. "This doesn't concern you, Billy. It's between me and your mother."

In one smooth motion that reminded Marcus of a mountain lion preparing to pounce, Billy uncrossed his legs, unclasped his hands, and leaned forward, folding his arms on Marcus's desk. "I beg your pardon, Colonel, but anything that concerns my mother concerns me."

Marcus had to admit Billy was right. Snowbird was his mother, therefore, his concern. Besides, the lad was tenacious in the way he looked out for her. Marcus respected that.

"I caught on to your little game a long time ago," Billy continued. "You're forgetting I was around when she wasn't. I've seen that lost look come over you when you thought no one was looking. What I don't understand is why you're doing this to her."

"Because, deep down, I know your mother really doesn't want to be here. She never would have come had it not been for my accident."

"You don't know what you're talking about."

"Yes, I do. I asked her to come."

"You asked her to come here to escape the removal. You never asked her to come as your wife."

Thinking back, Marcus frowned and realized Billy was right. He hadn't asked Snowbird to come as his wife. He'd just assumed she would never leave her people for any reason—including him. That still didn't change the reason she had finally come. "Look, Billy, before this happened"—he held up his half right arm—"I'd made arrangements to retire honorably and marry your mother. The accident took that choice away from me. It made me a disabled soldier instead." He shook his head. "I'll not allow it to take your mother's choices away from her. She belongs with her people. She's their leader."

Billy wagged his head. "As I said, you don't know what you're talking about."

Frustration mounting, Marcus leaned forward on his one whole arm until he was practically nose-to-nose with the kid. "Then please explain."

"She's no longer leader of our clan."

Shock blindsided Marcus, causing his head to jerk back. "What!"

"I said—"

"I know what you said." Dazed at first, Marcus stood and strode to his window, staring out at the darkness while he collected his thoughts. As he did, suspicions quickly moved in.

Swinging back around to face Billy, he narrowed his eyes. "What happened? Why is she no longer leader of her clan?"

"Because it was time to pass that responsibility down to Ethan. It was time for her to move on." He hesitated. "It was finally time for *her*."

Marcus wanted to believe Billy but was too afraid to allow hope back in. "When did this change in leadership take place?"

He shrugged a nonchalant shoulder. "After she received Emma's letter."

His floundering spirits died. "So my accident did have something to do with her decision to come here."

"Look, Colonel. I'm not going to sit here and argue with you over who's right or who's wrong. All I know is she was willing to leave her old life behind in order to be with you, just like you were willing to leave all this"—he made a sweeping motion with one hand—"to live in the wilderness with her before you had the accident.

"I hate to be the one to bruise your ego," Billy continued, "but Snowbird Walker is the smartest person I know. She's a lot more capable of deciding what's best for her than you are. But she's also human, and she has her limits. If you break her heart this time, you'll never get a chance to break it again." Rising, he picked his hat up off the desk. "That's a promise I'll personally see to myself."

Placing his hat on his head, he turned and ambled toward the door.

"Billy?" Marcus stopped him midstride. When the young man looked back, Marcus added, "I only want what's best for her."

"So do I." With that, he touched the brim of his hat and walked out of the room.

❧

Marcus stared at the door for a long time, trying to figure out what he should do. But his thoughts only became more confused and convoluted.

Finally, in desperation, he whispered, "Dear God, what should I do?"

Marcus's chin quivered. His heart pounded against his chest. Slowly, he closed his eyes as the first of many tears of shame slid down his cheek. What right did he have asking God for anything? Marcus had blamed Him for the accident that took his arm. Lashed out at Him in anger. Accused God of deserting him when, in reality, Marcus had been the deserter. And in the midst of his bitterness and anger, he'd rejected God's love—and the love of a priceless woman.

Humility rained down on Marcus and sent him first to his knees, then prostrate on the floor, his forehead resting on his one folded arm. "Oh, God, please forgive me. I am Your child, but I've strayed so far away from You. Will You ever allow me to come back? Will You ever allow me the feel Your sweet presence in my life once again?"

Marcus continued to pray on into the night, and in the wee hours, he felt the redemption and forgiveness he was seeking.

❧

Snowbird stood on the balcony of the bedroom she had occupied during her stay at the Gunter Plantation. Dew sparkled like white jewels sprinkled across the green grass. The robin sang her cheer-up song, and the bees searched for nectar among the roses in the garden below. She closed her eyes and drew in a deep breath of the sweet morning air. In her mind, she committed to memory a picture of the huge magnolia trees, sprawling oaks, and lacy cotton fields. She would miss this place, the land, and the people. For a while, it was her destiny. But Marcus was healed. She no longer had a reason to stay.

She had hoped things would turn out differently, that Marcus would want her to stay. But his actions over the past month had made it clear he didn't. And while her heart was breaking into a million pieces, she didn't regret her decision to come. She could leave with a sense of closure that she and Marcus would never be. Even though she still loved him with every fiber of her being, there was an odd measure of peace in knowing she could finally finish this chapter of her life and move on.

Opening her eyes, Snowbird looked up at the blue sky with its scattering of white, puffy clouds. "Thank You, Father, for giving me this peace beyond understanding."

❧

"Marcus?"

Marcus stopped pacing and looked up to where Snowbird

stood at the top of the stairs. Billy's protective hand circled her upper arm.

"I didn't expect to see you this morning," she said as she and Billy proceeded down the steps. "I thought you'd already be out and about your day."

"I must speak with you."

"All right."

As they reached the bottom of the stairs, Billy released her arm. "I'll go help Nelms load the carriage," he said.

At first Marcus couldn't speak but stood awestruck by the beauty that radiated from Snowbird's face. It wasn't physical or amorous, but it was pure and born of peace. It was serene.

Fear dampened his palm and tightened his chest. He clenched his fist. He thought she'd at least be a little disappointed about leaving. But she obviously wasn't. What if she no longer loved him? What if he'd waited too long, pushed her away one too many times?

"What's wrong, Marcus?" Reaching up, she touched her cheek. "Do I have something on my face?"

"No! No!" He captured her hand and, for a prayerful moment, closed his eyes while he held her fingers against his lips. "You're beautiful," he added, lowering their hands between them.

Her eyelids fluttered. Other than that, she didn't react but appeared to be trapped in a stony trance.

"I love you, Snowbird."

His words snapped her out of her frozen state. Pulling her hand away, she stepped back. "Marcus, don't."

He clung to her hand. "Snowbird, please don't tell me it's too late. Please hear me out."

She stopped her retreat and waited.

"I was an idiot to push you away."

He paused to consider his next words. He had to make each one count.

"Go on," she urged. "I'm listening."

"I thought the most important thing in your life was leading your people. I thought by pushing you away and making you think I could live a happy, full life without you, I was giving you back your freedom. The last thing I wanted was for you to tie yourself down to a cripple out of some sense of duty and obligation."

"It was never about duty or obligation, Marcus. Couldn't you see that?"

"No. I couldn't. I was too wrapped up in my own self-pity and misery to see or feel anything else."

Skepticism lingered in her eyes. "What brought about this sudden change of heart?"

"God. Allowing Him back into my life. Of course, a little man-to-man talk your son had with me started me thinking I was about to let the best thing that ever happened to me walk out of my life for good."

He released her hand and laid his single palm against her face. "Please, Snowbird. Please forgive me and give me another chance. It doesn't matter where we are, in the valley, here, in a cave—I don't care where we live as long as we live and serve God together."

The doubt dissipated from her eyes. Serenity returned. "Yes."

He couldn't breathe. He hadn't expected her answer to come this soon. He'd expected her to want to take some time to consider his proposal. "Yes?" he repeated, just to make sure he hadn't misunderstood.

"Yes, I'll marry you, and I'll live here with you. Your people will be my people and your home, my home." She smiled a radiant smile. "Your God, my God."

As she stepped into his embrace, Marcus realized she was giving him a gift that couldn't be measured or comprehended by the human mind—the gift of unconditional love. It was there the day they met, and it would be there beyond death. It was the reason she had not hesitated, the reason she'd been so forgiving.

Only One could love greater—the heavenly Father.

"I love you, Marcus Gunter. I'm so glad you came to your senses."

"So am I, my love. So am I."

Drawing back, he framed one side of her face with his hand. "Can we get married soon?"

"How does next week sound to you?"

"Too far away, but I guess it'll have to do."

fifteen

My dearest daughter, Emily,

By the time you receive this letter, I will be married to your father. We will make our home here in Virginia, at his plantation.

As you know, after your father delivered your children to you, he planned to return to the Blue Haven and claim my hand in marriage. Unfortunately, he encountered an accident along the way, which cost him his right arm. Not wanting me to tie myself to a "cripple," he wrote to me and told me he no longer wanted to marry me and was returning to his home in Virginia. At first, I accepted this, until your aunt Emma wrote and told me Marcus wasn't progressing in his recovery and needed me. So I turned over leadership of our clan to your brother and came.

I know that will come as a surprise to you. After all, two years ago I couldn't see myself doing anything else with my life but leading our people back to freedom. But it was a passion fed in part by my hate and anger toward the white men. Once I allowed God back into my life, I saw He had a different plan for me. I'm also finding the days satisfying and fulfilling here, not boring or tedious as I once thought life on a plantation among servants would be. Just yesterday, one of the workers on the plantation sent word to the main house that his daughter had taken an unrelenting case of dysentery and needed a physician. While we waited for the doctor to come, I prepared a tea from the bark of the wild cherry trees that grow along the boundaries of the plantation property. I am delighted to report the child's fever broke later that night, and, by the time the doctor arrived, she was sitting up in her bed, asking for teacakes.

After those drunken men attacked me in the woods near our home almost nineteen years ago, I allowed my sorrow and anger to quench my desire to help people with the gift God had given me. But He has given me a second chance to serve Him not only with my gift and my life but also with Marcus. Now Ethan is leading our people in the East, as he should be, and you are married to a wonderful man and serving our people who now live west of the Mississippi. While I miss you both more than words can say, I am exceedingly grateful my family has chosen to serve God in such rewarding and prosperous ways.

So many times, Emily, I think of the journey that brought me here—the one that started twenty-nine years ago at that little mission school in Spring Place. I deeply regret that you and your brother had to grow up not knowing your father. While I know you and Ethan have forgiven me, it is still a sorrow I will always have to live with. Yet I often wonder if our marriage would have been a happy one had we married at such a tender age. Marcus and I were both such different people then, driven by such different causes. If the trials have served to make me stronger and more willing to love unconditionally, then I thank God for each and every one of them.

Snowbird paused in writing and looked out the window beyond her writing desk, where a gentle breeze tugged a few fading dogwood leaves from their branches. She still couldn't believe she was going to be married today to the man she'd fallen in love with twenty-nine years ago. She thought back to the life-altering events of her past: the betrayal of Marcus's parents, the births of her children and grandchildren, the attack that had left her physical body scarred, the loss of a land she once thought she couldn't live without, the loss of Marcus's right arm. There had been joy among the sorrow. There had been laughter and there had been pain—pain so great that, at times, she thought she would die, had wanted to die.

But she realized now there had also been grace. Amazing grace, redeeming grace molding both her and Marcus into the people they were now. Not perfect by any measure, but willing to serve God and each other with confidence that they were both where they were supposed to be, entering a new season of their lives, with Him as their center. Reaching up, she wiped a tear of joy from her face.

A knock sounded on the door. Before Snowbird could answer, Nettie opened the door and came in with her arms full of two elaborate gowns. When she met Snowbird's gaze, Nettie stopped short. "Why, Miz Snowbird, what you be cryin' for? This is your wedding day. The happiest day of your life, and one you been waitin' on for a long, long time."

Snowbird smiled. "Oh, Nettie, these are tears of joy. Besides the day I pledged my life to God, this is the happiest day of my life."

Nettie returned an understanding smile. "We got the alterations made on these two dresses." She held them up. "Miss Emma said the green, but I think the yellow will suit your style better."

Snowbird saw why Nettie thought the yellow would be

the appropriate choice. The green gown, Emma's pick, had a lower neckline. While still modest, the gown had a neckline low enough to reveal the scars just below Snowbird's neck. The yellow gown had a high collar that would button to Snowbird's chin.

"Thank you, Nettie," Snowbird said, "I appreciate you looking out for me. But the green gown will do just fine."

Nettie laughed out loud. "Then let's get you dressed."

Snowbird reached for the green gown. "That's all right. I can manage."

The maid fanned Snowbird's hand away. "I'm sure you can, but you just stand there and do as I tells you. Let Miz Nettie do what the good Lord called her to do."

Snowbird complied. This was a part of her life she'd have a problem adjusting to. As Nettie started humming a cheerful tune, Snowbird realized the maid was doing what God had called her to do and with gladness.

Once she had dressed and Nettie had left the room, Snowbird finished her letter to Emily, placed it in a parchment envelope, and laid it on her writing desk next to the letter addressed to Ethan. Now she was ready to get married.

≈

"Is my collar buttoned? Is my vest straight? Perhaps I should wear the brown coat instead of the black."

"Your collar is buttoned. Your vest is straight. And the black coat is a better choice than the brown," came Billy's calm voice.

Marcus turned from the oval mirror to look at his soon-to-be stepson. How could the young man be so relaxed? Nothing seemed to bother him. "Have you seen your mother today? Is she all right? Is she as nervous as I?"

Billy pushed away from the wall he was leaning on, picked the black jacket up from where it lay across the bed, and sauntered across the room. He held the coat out for Marcus. As Marcus started to slip his whole arm through the sleeve, Billy said, "I did see Mother earlier this morning. She said her feet were getting cold."

Confused, Marcus stopped and blinked at Billy. Then, as the meaning behind the young man's words crystallized, his mouth dropped open.

"Relax, Colonel." Billy grinned. "I'm just having some fun."

Marcus sighed. Some of the tenseness left his shoulders. "Honestly, I never know what to expect from you. I'm so glad you're here. You help keep us all sane."

While Marcus adjusted his jacket, Billy stepped back and tucked his hands into his own coat pockets. "Thank you—I think."

"Trust me. That's a compliment."

Silence fell between the two men, and Marcus suspected Billy wanted to say something. "I promise I'll take good care of your mother, Billy."

"I know. Otherwise, we wouldn't still be here." He chewed his lower lip. "I want to thank you for the job."

"You're quite welcome. You're an intelligent young man and a hard worker. You'll be a tremendous help to me in overseeing the cotton production."

"I also want to ask you something."

Marcus stopped inspecting his clothing and gave his full attention to Billy.

"You know, I don't have a father," Billy continued. "At least not an earthly father." He hesitated.

Marcus nodded.

"I wonder. . .I mean. . .would you mind if I called you *Pop*?"

Tears blurred Marcus's vision. He'd expected *Marcus*, or even *Father*. But *Pop*? Billy could not have given a greater compliment. "Of course," he said, his voice raspy with emotion. "I'd like that. I'd like that very much." He extended his hand. Instead of accepting it, Billy gathered Marcus up in a brief, hearty hug, then left the room.

Marcus stared at the door for a moment. Could this really be happening? Not only was he about to marry the woman he'd waited for all his life, but he'd also just been given the gift of another son. The tears of happiness pooling in his eyes spilled over to his face. Vigorously he wiped them away. He didn't want to mess up his shirt.

He strolled to the window and looked out over the rolling hills of the plantation. He thought of how life had once beaten him down, and how God had renewed his strength. *Thank You, Father, for giving me a second chance with You and with the woman I love.*

A knock sounded at the door. "Come in."

Marcus turned as Frederick entered the room. "Are you ready, my friend?" the minister asked.

Calmness settled over Marcus, banishing his frayed nerves. He nodded. "I'm ready."

❧

"You look beautiful, Mother."

Out of habit, Snowbird raised a hand to her neck.

"Don't." Billy walked across her dressing room, to where she stood beside the mirror.

"Are you never going to stop dragging your feet, Billy?"

He smiled his infectious smile. "Are you never going to stop being a mother, even on your wedding day?" He captured her hand and held it between them.

"No. I will never stop being your mother."

"Good."

"I hope you can someday come to think of Marcus as your father."

A mischievous light sparkled in his eyes. He motioned his head toward the door and held out his arm to her. "Come on. We don't want to keep Pop waiting."

"Pop?" She blinked. "You called him *Pop*."

Billy shrugged a shoulder but offered no explanation. And Snowbird didn't need one. She tucked her hand in the arm her son offered and walked toward the door.

Thirty minutes later, as Snowbird walked down the aisle of the plantation chapel alongside her son, she was overcome by a sense of completeness. After twenty-nine years, her family was about to become whole.

Frederick performed the nuptials. Emma and the rest of the plantation residents all served as witnesses.

When the minister said, "You may now kiss your bride," Marcus did, and nearly three decades melted away into a constant, steady river of joy that would never run dry.

Then without further ado, Marcus said, "Hang on," to his bride. As she wrapped her arms around his neck, he braced his half arm beneath her shoulders and his left arm beneath her knees. With boisterous laughter bubbling up from his chest, he picked her up and carried her out of the church.

A Letter To Our Readers

Dear Reader:

In order that we might better contribute to your reading enjoyment, we would appreciate your taking a few minutes to respond to the following questions. We welcome your comments and read each form and letter we receive. When completed, please return to the following:

Fiction Editor
Heartsong Presents
PO Box 719
Uhrichsville, Ohio 44683

1. Did you enjoy reading *Bittersweet Remembrance* by Gina Fields?
   ❑ Very much! I would like to see more books by this author!
   ❑ Moderately. I would have enjoyed it more if

   _____

   _____

   _____

2. Are you a member of **Heartsong Presents**? ❑ Yes ❑ No
   If no, where did you purchase this book? _____

   _____

3. How would you rate, on a scale from 1 (poor) to 5 (superior), the cover design? _____

4. On a scale from 1 (poor) to 10 (superior), please rate the following elements.

   ____ Heroine   ____ Plot
   ____ Hero   ____ Inspirational theme
   ____ Setting   ____ Secondary characters

5. These characters were special because? _____

_____

_____

6. How has this book inspired your life? _____

_____

_____

7. What settings would you like to see covered in future
   Heartsong Presents books? _____

_____

_____

8. What are some inspirational themes you would like to see
   treated in future books? _____

_____

_____

9. Would you be interested in reading other **Heartsong
   Presents** titles? ❑ Yes ❑ No

10. Please check your age range:
    ❑ Under 18   ❑ 18-24
    ❑ 25-34   ❑ 35-45
    ❑ 46-55   ❑ Over 55

Name _____

Occupation _____

Address _____

City, State, Zip _____

Minnesota Brothers

4 stories in 1

The Nilsson family has decided to settle in Minnesota, where each brother seeks a wife. Can a family's faith sustain romance?

Titles by author Lena Nelson Dooley include: *The Other Brother*, *His Brother's Castoff*, *Double Deception*, and *Gerda's Lawman*

Historical, paperback, 464 pages, 5³⁄₁₆" x 8"

Please send me ____ copies of *Minnesota Brothers*. I am enclosing $6.97 for each. (Please add $2.00 to cover postage and handling per order. OH add 7% tax.)

Send check or money order, no cash or C.O.D.s, please.

Name _____

Address _____

City, State, Zip _____

To place a credit card order, call 1-740-922-7280.

Send to: Heartsong Presents Readers' Service, PO Box 721, Uhrichsville, OH 44683

Presents

Great Inspirational Romance at a Great Price!

Heartsong Presents books are inspirational romances in contemporary and historical settings, designed to give you an enjoyable, spirit-lifting reading experience. You can choose wonderfully written titles from some of today's best authors like Peggy Darty, Sally Laity, DiAnn Mills, Colleen L. Reece, Debra White Smith, and many others.

When ordering quantities less than twelve, above titles are $2.97 each.
Not all titles may be available at time of order.

SEND TO: **Heartsong Presents** Reader's Service
P.O. Box 721, Uhrichsville, Ohio 44683

Please send me the items checked above. I am enclosing $ _____
(please add $2.00 to cover postage per order. OH add 7% tax. NJ add 6%). Send check or money order, no cash or C.O.D.s, please.
To place a credit card order, call 1-740-922-7280.

NAME _____

ADDRESS _____

CITY/STATE _____ ZIP_____